PUSHED TOO FAR

PUSHED TOO FAR

Copyright © 2012 by Ann Voss Peterson

Cover and art copyright © 2012 by Carl Graves

First Edition: June 2012

PUSHED TOO FAR

A THRILLER

ANN VOSS PETERSON

To Barbra

INTRODUCTION

As a reader, there is nothing I love more than the chill of a cold, atmospheric thriller. It's why I've seen the film FARGO and read Scott B. Smith's classic A SIMPLE PLAN more times than I care to admit. It's the icy claustrophobia of the small-town Midwest in the dead of winter, that when channeled right, makes for something special—the best crime fiction in the world.

This standalone novel by Ann Voss Peterson, PUSHED TOO FAR, is that kind of special, and its heroine, Val Ryker, Chief of Police of tiny Lake Loyal, Wisconsin, is one for the ages. When the victim of a prior murder that rocked the village inexplicably turns up, the man incarcerated for her killing, an undisputed monster, is released from prison with a hell of a grudge, intent on holding Ryker and everything she loves to the fire.

PUSHED TOO FAR is not only a first-rate thriller, not only a police-procedural written with absolute authority by a writer who knows her stuff, but most of all, most importantly, it's a portrait of Police Chief Ryker, a woman of extraordinary courage who is pushed beyond her breaking point.

Good thrillers put their characters through the wringer. Great ones rain down holy hell upon their heads—physically, emotionally, psychologically—and aren't satisfied until the reader is spent, exhilarated, terrified, and lavishly entertained.

This is a great thriller, and with it, Peterson has firmly established herself as a major league talent and a must-read writer.

Enjoy!

Blake Crouch, March 2012

Chapter
One

David Lund had trained for this moment and visualized it a thousand times. But his legs still vibrated as he toed off his shoes and pushed a stocking foot into yellow rubber.

He shook the thermal suit and worked his foot deeper, finally seating it into the attached boot. Shoving his other foot home, then pulling the suit up his torso, he squinted at the skin of ice covering much of Lake Loyal.

He couldn't see a damn thing.

Not a spot of colorful clothing, not a dark shape against the flat expanse of gray. But a police officer on a routine patrol of the park reported a woman had fallen through the ice. And she wouldn't last long. Not in Wisconsin's early December chill.

He had to hurry.

Activity buzzed around him, fellow firefighters, EMTs, cops yelling out orders, getting into position. They all had their role, a well-oiled machine.

He only hoped it would be enough.

Lund shimmied his shoulders into the suit, tucked in his sweatshirt, and pulled the hood over his head. The rubber was meant to fit tightly, to protect him from frigid water. Once finished dressing, he'd be encased in yellow and black, only his eyes and nose showing. He could float in the lake for hours, buoyed by the air left in the suit, his own body heat protecting him from the chill.

Of course, getting into the damn thing was a trick bordering on magic.

Dempsey and Johnson raced past, carrying the pontoon raft from Unit One to shore, their boots crunching on the frozen pea gravel path circling the lake. Wind thrashed leafless trees and spun the merry-go-round in the park, as if it were ridden by ghosts.

Lund raised the zipper as high up his chest as he could, then stuffed his arms into the sleeves.

The newest addition to the Lake Loyal PD, a part-time cop named Schoenborn, ran up the sloping shoreline toward him, her cheeks pink with the cold.

"You see her?" he asked. "I can't from here."

"You'll spot her when you get on the water. She's just on the other side of that clump of cattails. I haven't seen her move." Her voice soared to a higher pitch than usual, making the rookie seem even younger than Lund suspected she was.

"You the first one here?"

"Yeah." Wind tore a few dark strands from her ponytail and whipped them across her face. "After I called it in, all I could do was wait. I've never felt so useless in my life."

Lund had tasted that feeling more often than he wanted to admit. He'd like to tell her it would be all right, but sometimes people couldn't be saved, no matter how much you wanted it, no matter how hard you tried. If anyone knew that, it was him.

He pushed his hands into the attached rubber mitts and eyed the cop. "If you want to feel useful, you can help zip me up."

She sprang toward the zipper and worked on tugging and tucking until it was up to his neck.

A second later, Dempsey joined them, lending his experienced hands to the task. "Okay, let's get some of this air out, and you're good to go."

Lund crouched into a ball, the suit puffing up around him like a balloon.

The weathered firefighter patted him down, pushing out the extra air. He snugged the zipper the remaining inches over Lund's chin, pulling the rubber hood tight around his face until only his nose and eyes were exposed to the cold. "That's as good as it's going to get."

Lund stood, the suit sucking to him like thick plastic wrap. His breath rasped in his ears, the sound magnified by the hood.

Dempsey clipped the tow rope to Lund's back, and he started down to shore feeling every ridge and bump of the frozen ground through the rubber boots, as if walking outside in socks. He stepped carefully. A tear would only slow him down, force him to start over with another suit, and he had no time to lose.

The woman couldn't last long in the freezing water. Her body would shut down, muscles refusing to move, reflexes slowing until she could no longer stay afloat and sank under the slushy waves.

But in cold water, drowning didn't necessarily mean death.

For about an hour after breathing stopped, maybe more, she could be rescued and revived without suffering brain damage. Lund wasn't sure how long the victim had been in the lake, but if there was a chance of pulling her out within that golden hour, he would grab it.

The ice rimming the lake was thick enough to support weight, and Lund skidded out to the spot where the pontoon raft rested. A tow rope connected it to the firefighters on shore, just like the one on his belt, enabling Dempsey and Johnson to tow him back once he had secured the woman to the raft.

Until then, it was up to him.

The rescue craft was made up of two foam board pontoons with an aluminum tube rail running along each. Leaning forward, he grasped the rails, stepped into the space between, and shuffled over the ice, carrying the raft as if driving Fred Flintstone's car.

Twenty feet from open water the surface started to creak beneath his feet.

He took a step, then another, his third plunged through, water over the ankle.

He lifted onto the raft, straddling the open water and bracing the outsides of his knees against the rails. The lake rolled and shifted under him, chunks of ice and swirls of water. He grabbed the paddle from its clamp and dug into the slush between bright orange pontoons, moving out into the lake.

Squinting against the wind, he could see her now, between the remnants of cattails and open water, just where the cop had indicated. Light pink jacket. Long brown hair encrusted with ice. The victim wasn't moving—no flailing, no struggling—just lying face down in the water, bobbing with the movement of the waves.

Shit.

He paddled hard, the burn settling into his arms, his shoulders. Shifting side to side, he used his weight to steer toward the woman like a kid riding a skateboard.

Unconscious?

Dead?

How much time had passed since she entered the water? What in the hell had she been doing this far out on thin ice?

Sweat slicked his back. His throat ached with the chill air, his ears, his jaw. He pushed his muscles, closing the last few yards.

A foot or two away, he fitted the paddle back into the clamps and moved to the front of the pontoons. He grabbed the nylon straps at the front of the craft with one hand and reached for the woman with the other.

His awkward, rubber mitts slipped off her head, her shoulder.

He tried again.

On his third attempt, he snagged a hank of hair and pulled her toward the craft. Scooping his hands under, he coaxed her torso to rotate.

Her face tilted skyward.

Pale skin. Blue lips. White eyes staring into the overcast sky.

Lund's legs started to shake.

He couldn't move. He couldn't think. He could only stare.

His wife had died two years ago. Her body burned until there was nothing left but shattered bone and ashes.

And yet here she was, staring up at him from the icy water, her beautiful face frozen in a scream.

Chapter
Two

To say Val Ryker was worried would be a vast pile of understatement.

Arriving at the lake, she marched past the vacant swing set and down the pea gravel trail. She worked her right hand as she walked, flexing and stretching, trying to coax feeling back into her fingertips, even though she knew it wouldn't work. It never did.

But that wasn't what concerned her. Not right now.

Her sergeant's voice had sounded strained on the phone, unusual coming from a man only one degree more expressive than a brick wall. And although he refused to give details, she'd ducked out of the village's Christmas tree lighting ceremony as soon as Grace had finished her solo and raced to Rossum Park, going as fast as she dared without lights and siren.

A handful of volunteer firefighters milled at lake's edge, along with Baker and Caruthers of the EMS. She didn't want to talk to anyone, not until she knew what had prompted Olson's call. Squinting into the wind, she scanned the lake until she spotted the sergeant's towering bulk.

Up to his knees in frozen green-brown grass and the naked spears of cattails, Olson waved her onto the ice, the motion stiff and abrupt. The sheen of sweat slicked his brow, yet his ears were red with cold.

She picked her way across the slick surface. "Sergeant? What is it?"

He looked up but didn't answer, as if waiting for her to get closer.

Unease lodged under her rib cage like a bad meal. The fire department's ice rescue raft rested at Olson's feet, neon orange, the trail where it had been dragged out of the open water, over ice and along the edge of the cattails reflected the gray sky.

Then she saw the body.

Female. Strapped to the front of the pontoon raft. Her head and shoulders propped up as if she was lounging on a pillow. She wore a pink coat and jeans and her mouth was open, as if taking a last gasp for breath. Worst of all, her skin held the pallor of frozen chicken and her hair stuck in an icy mat to the side of her face, obscuring her features.

Val was aware of the call that had come into dispatch. A woman had fallen through the ice, drowned. It was a tragedy they'd failed to rescue her, but that didn't explain why Olson had called her away from the Christmas tree lighting or what had made him so upset.

"She's dead," he said, once Val reached him.

"I can see that. She looks frozen solid. I wonder how long she was in the water before the call came in."

"She's dead," he gave her a pointed look, "for the second time."

"Come again?"

"Take a look at her face. A good look."

Having started her career in the Chicago PD, Val had seen bodies before, more of them than she cared to think about.

Even since she'd moved to small town Wisconsin, she'd had a few occasions to face death—people who refused to strap on their seat belts splattered across pavement, the depressed man who'd decided to clean his teeth with the barrel of a shotgun—but she had to admit, human popsicle was a new one.

Preparing herself to face another death, Val leaned over the body.

Beneath the frozen hair, the victim's eyes were nearly as white as her skin, their original color nearly impossible to guess. But she was pretty. High cheekbones, full lips, and a mole on her right jaw.

God help her.

Val closed her eyes, then opened them, but the face remained the same. One she'd never forget. One that sent shudders through her, head to toe. "This isn't possible."

Olson stepped beside her, pulled off his hat and rubbed a hand over the blond stubble he called hair. "Where has she been all this time? And who was the body in the barrel?"

Questions she couldn't answer.

She let out a heavy breath that condensed in the air before being whipped away by the wind.

About two years ago, she'd spent countless hours searching for Kelly Ann Lund, the thirty-three-year-old daughter of a local dairy farmer. After shards of her bones were discovered in the farm's burning barrel, Val had spent countless more tracking down the man who'd murdered her and putting him in prison.

And now Kelly Ann was staring up at them, not burned in the least.

Olson finally broke the silence. "So much for DNA."

"Mito DNA," she reminded. Unlike nuclear DNA, mitochondrial DNA wasn't unique to one person, but to a maternal line. Passed down from mother to offspring, it could belong to any of Kelly's maternal relations.

Olson scuffed the ice with the toe of one boot. "She doesn't have an evil twin, does she?"

Val appreciated the attempt at levity, but she couldn't manage a smile. A sergeant at the time, she'd been lead investigator on the case. The facts were burned into her memory. The bones recovered belonged to a female. The mito DNA indicated the victim was part of Kelly's maternal line. And yet … "She had no siblings at all. No living maternal relatives. That's why I was so sure it was her."

"We were all sure."

She gave Olson a grateful glance.

"We need to call the chief."

She tried not to feel the sting of his words. "I'm the chief, Pete."

"Sorry. Schneider. We need to call Schneider."

Jeff Schneider had been a mentor, almost a father figure, to them both. Of course unlike Val, Pete had spent his entire career working his way up through the ranks of the tiny Lake Loyal PD. Val knew he'd assumed he would take over as chief when Schneider retired. The whole town had assumed.

Then she'd arrested the brutal murderer of Kelly Ann Lund, and the job was hers—first female police chief of the village of Lake Loyal.

She pulled out her cell phone.

"He'll know what to do," Olson said.

"I'm not calling Schneider. I'm calling Harlan." At least this late in the afternoon, it wasn't likely the coroner was up to his elbows in a dead body, not that that would faze the delusional old Casanova. "No point in moving forward until we have an official ID."

"Maybe we don't have to get an ID." Olson's voice was so low, she could barely hear it over the wind. He squinted toward the shoreline. "I secured the scene as soon as she was brought in. No one's gotten a good look at her. No one except Lund."

"David Lund?"

"He was the one who towed her in."

She glanced toward shore and spotted Kelly's estranged husband for the first time. He sat a few feet from the truck, one hip hitched up on the edge of a playground structure, cradling a steaming foam cup in his hands. He still wore the neon yellow suit the firefighters used for ice rescue. Hood peeled back, he watched them, the wind ruffling his dark, wavy hair.

"I know it's a crazy idea. Probably stupid. That's why we need to talk to the chief."

Val forced her focus back to Olson. "What idea?"

"Like I said, no one else has seen her. No one knows it's Kelly." He stared straight at Val, as if willing her to understand. A muscle along his jaw flexed.

"Pete ..."

"We say we can't ID her, not local, fell in the lake."

"I don't think you should say anything more."

"You don't think Kelly ending up in the lake is an accident, do you? That she just happened to be strolling over ice so thin even the most rabid ice fishermen haven't put up a single shanty?"

She didn't have to glance around to note the public park and forest preserve, the upscale houses rimming the lake, the Shoreline Supper Club overlooking the expanse of water and ice. The park was well used in the summer, but even in winter, a number of people walked area trails and gazed out over the beautiful vista.

Not to mention the fact that an officer checked Rossum Park in the afternoon and once after midnight on routine patrol. Kelly hadn't been in the water during the midnight check, not that the officer could see. But in the light of day, there she was. "Obviously she was supposed to be found," Val said.

"And the one person it helps is serving time in Waupun. You know what's going to happen as soon as his lawyer hears we found Kelly's body."

She knew. Her head pounded with it.

Guilty verdicts weren't something one could transfer from body to body like a change of clothing. She'd arrested Dixon Hess for killing Kelly Lund—the witness seeing them together, rumors of an affair, her blood in his truck; that was the evidence that tied him to those charred bones. Without Kelly as the glue, Val's whole case disintegrated.

"Forty-eight hours. That's all we'll have," Olson said.

She felt sick to her stomach. About Kelly Ann's death, about the prospect of a killer going free, about the fact that Olson could even suggest they decimate every ethical standard and break the law themselves to fight back. "We'll make our case, but we'll follow the law."

"We don't even have a fucking clue who he burned." Olson looked away and took several breaths. Turning back, he lowered his voice. "Our job is to serve and protect the people of Lake Loyal. You think letting a monster loose is the way to go about that?"

"We're officers of the law. We have to follow the law."

"And if we aren't able to come up with a new case against him, he goes free. Just like he did in Omaha."

She shook her head, remembering the horror of the Omaha case, the poor girl he tortured, the case that should have been a slam dunk. "If the Omaha police had played everything by the book, he would have been convicted."

"You don't know that." Olson twisted his stocking cap in his hands, and Val had to wonder if it was a stand in for her throat. "There was a lot of evidence against him. It should have been enough, even with the illegal search of his car."

She couldn't disagree. Even now she could hear echoes of the Omaha PD Lieutenant's anguish when she'd called about the case.

"He was the worst I've ever known," said the thirty-five year veteran. *"The cruelest man I've ever seen."*

"We'll stop him." Her voice sounded weaker than she'd wanted, and she straightened her spine to compensate.

Lips in a hard line, Olson looked past her and focused on the shoreline. "You better be right."

She followed his gaze.

A white van drove through the parking lot and past the playground equipment, the logo of a local television station emblazoned on its side.

Great.

Once the media sank their teeth into this, there was no going back. Hess's attorney would file a habeas corpus motion and the clock would start ticking.

Forty eight hours.

It was all the time she had, and it wasn't enough.

Not nearly enough.

Chapter
Three

Dale Kasdorf wasn't surprised when he saw police and fire trucks and ambulances stream into the park. If anything, he wondered why it took them so long.

He trudged down the ridge in the adjacent forest preserve. Dressed in snow camo, he couldn't be seen today any more than he had been last night, and that was good with him. Nothing came of talking to cops. Nothing but harassment.

He'd learned his lesson the first time.

Approaching his traps, he spotted the news truck. For a while he just stood and watched them unload the camera, set up the reporter, get ready to intercept the pretty blond police chief when she reached shore. Apparently they'd tell the story on the news tonight—or at least they'd try—but he wouldn't watch.

He knew the story better than they did.

He continued, checking each of his four traps. Two rabbits. One for freezing, one for eating. A good day. Maybe he'd use the fur to make a hat. Get real Native American and use all the parts of the kill.

He liked that idea.

After bagging his game, he reset the traps in different spots, far from the smells of blood and struggle that would surely scare off the next round of game. In summer, it was hard to utilize the forest preserve without some kid or dog stumbling on the steel jaws and ripping their damn fool legs apart. But after deer season ended, people left the woods to the rabbits and squirrels, foxes and coyotes.

And to him.

The way he liked it.

Ready to head back to his place and cook up some stew, he took one last glance at the lake below. His eyes skimmed over the young female cop collecting trash along water's edge and found the bright orange raft, the body strapped to it barely visible in the long grass reaching through ice.

He'd seen a woman die early this morning. That had to be marked.

But he wasn't going to tell this time. Not a goddamn word. Because the only thing worse than being a victim in this world was being a witness.

And he would never make that mistake again.

Lund had lived through a lot of bad days, but this one might be the worst.

He'd barely moved since he'd pulled Kelly to stable ice. Hadn't been able to face taking off the thermal suit, as if the clinging rubber was the only thing keeping him from shattering into a million pieces.

She'd died two years ago, and his failure to save her still stung like an open wound. Still he'd pulled himself together. He'd gotten through the investigation, the trial, and the months of nothingness after.

Now he had to face it again.

He watched the police chief pick her way over the ice. She was a beautiful woman, high cheekbones and serious, gray eyes. If he'd met her under other circumstances, he was sure his attraction would be his focus. Instead, every time he saw her, he felt raw and wary.

She would want to talk to him, not just about the failed rescue today but where he'd been this morning, what he'd done last night, and it would all start over.

The news crew met her as soon as she'd stepped onto shore, camera heading her off, microphone pushed into her face. He could read her lips from here.

No comment.

No comment.

"You done with the suit?" Dempsey tromped up next to him and held out a hand.

Lund pushed himself up from the playground equipment and forced himself to peel off the protective layer. "I can take care of it."

"You did the paddling."

"You drove."

Dempsey shot him a sideways look. "Just give me the suit."

Lund handed it over. He knew Dempsey and Johnson were just trying to share the load. They didn't get that helping pack up wasn't a burden. On the contrary, being able to do something might help get his mind off Kelly, off the police chief and her inevitable questions.

Of course, he hadn't told his fellow firefighters exactly who he'd pulled from the water. Pete Olson had insisted he keep that information quiet, and now he was glad he'd listened. Dempsey and Johnson were coddling him enough just thinking he'd failed to save a woman he didn't know.

Too bad it wouldn't stay a secret for long. As soon as they found out, they would start treating him like he was as fragile as the ice on that lake.

Covering an area of rural land and small towns, the fire district didn't have a live-in firehouse. It had only two full-time firefighters, the chief, who handled the administrative end, and the fire inspector/community outreach director, who happened to be Lund. The rest were paid volunteers who trained regularly and responded to the radios they kept in their homes.

But the lack of other full-time firefighters wouldn't prevent the chief from insisting he take some time off, leaving him with nothing to do but sit around and think.

He looked back toward Police Chief Ryker. One last no comment, and she broke away from the camera and started his way.

He yanked on his boots, stood and tried his best to relax. He'd been through this drill before, knew what was coming, but that didn't mean he had a clue how to handle it. Or that he ever would.

"Mr. Lund. I'm glad I caught you." She skirted the ambulance and Unit One, wind streaming her blond hair across her face despite her efforts to push it away. She wore a dark wool coat over police blues, as usual, something that always struck him as odd compared to most chiefs of police who tended to prefer suits. He suspected she counted on the uniform to remind citizens of her authority, to give her an edge.

Not that she needed it.

Stopping in front of him, she shoved one hand in her pocket and studied him as if reading his mind. "This must be a shock. I'm so sorry."

The first time Kelly had been murdered he'd spent so much time studying Val Ryker's expressions, he no longer needed subtitles. "But you need to ask me a few questions."

"Unfortunately, yes."

"Seems last time the only answer you'd accept was a confession."

Her lips tightened. "Do you have something to confess?"

"I didn't kill her, and I don't know where she's been all this time. Will that suffice?"

"That's a start."

"You want to know where I was the past few hours and who can vouch for me."

She didn't answer, just waited for him to go on.

"I've been at the fire station all day, plenty of witnesses."

"And last night?"

"At the fire station late. Then I stopped at the Doghouse for a beer."

"After that?"

"Home alone, in bed. No witnesses. Not unless you count the Playboy channel."

Her expression didn't change.

He'd thrown in the Playboy channel to unnerve her, but it hadn't been a lie. Cable was as close as he'd gotten to a date in the two and a half years since Kelly declared she needed a break from their marriage. Except for work, it was the closest he'd gotten to a life.

"You didn't see or hear from Kelly?"

"No." He thought about last night. Coming home late, tired, maybe a little buzzed. The door swinging open before he'd inserted the key. "But someone might have been in my house."

Her eyebrows arched. "Did you report the break in?"

"I don't know if it was a break in. I'm pretty sure I locked the door, but I might have forgotten."

"Was anything missing?"

"Not that I could tell."

"I'll send someone over."

He shouldn't have mentioned it. Now he'd given the chief an excuse to poke around in his house. "Since nothing is missing, I don't think that's necessary, do you?"

Another arch of the brows. "It will only take a few minutes."

He'd been right. It was happening again. Kelly was dead, and he was the number one suspect. Everything he'd thought he'd put behind him was replaying like a recurring nightmare.

"It doesn't have to be so hard, you know."

He frowned. Now she really was reading his mind. "What are you suggesting? That I turn myself in?"

"Should you?"

"I didn't do anything."

"Then help me."

Out of all the things he expected Val Ryker to say, that wasn't one. "Help you with what?"

"The other body, the woman we believed was Kelly; we have to figure out who she really was."

He narrowed his eyes. She seemed serious. "I don't think I can do a better job of identifying her than DNA can."

"The type of DNA that was used for identification has some limitations."

At the time of the trial, the prosecutor, Monica Forbes, had explained to him the ins and outs of mitochondrial DNA. He'd only half listened, never dreaming the body could be anyone but Kelly. "I gave her a funeral. I buried her in my wife's grave. That's all I can tell you."

She took a controlled breath. "I think you can tell me more than that."

"I didn't kill her."

"Then cooperate. The body we found wasn't Kelly, but mito DNA and the bones themselves indicate it does belong to a female in her family."

"You looked at her family the first time around. I sat through the trial. Everyone it could have been was already dead."

"We obviously missed someone." She searched his eyes, as if the answer might be there.

Suddenly he was aware of every twitch of his face muscles, every shift of his gaze, every movement of his body. He had nothing to hide, yet at the same time, he couldn't help wondering what she was seeing. "If you're counting on me to solve this for you, you're shit out of luck."

She nodded, although whether that meant she accepted his answer or had plans to approach him in another way remained to be seen.

"We need to exhume the body we thought was Kelly's. It would be quickest if I could get your permission."

Digging up those bones shouldn't bother him. After all, he didn't even know who they belonged to. But a dull ache seized his chest, and he couldn't help feeling exhuming those bones was the last detail that made the whole mess real.

Kelly had died all over again.

And once again, he hadn't been able to save her.

"I know this is tough."

He shook his head. He didn't expect her concern, and he didn't want it. "Where do I sign?"

"I'll take you to the police station."

He shook his head. There wasn't a chance he was getting into a cop car with her. "I have my own ride." He gestured to Unit One.

"Suit yourself. But I need your signature as soon as possible. I'll make sure a release form is ready for you at the dispatcher's window."

"Fine."

She stared directly into his eyes, and for a moment, he felt more uncomfortable than he ever had under her interrogations. "Thanks for your help. I appreciate it."

His help.

Go figure. In the years he'd been married to Kelly, he'd never found a way to help her. And now? He wasn't sure if he was truly helping her or just harming himself.

He felt himself nod regardless. "I'll give you whatever you need."

Chapter
Four

By the time Val had gotten the release form signed by
David Lund, obtained a court order, notified the cemetery and gotten the go ahead from church leaders and
health department alike, the sun had disappeared behind the bluffs to the west. Pushing the exhumation to
first thing the next morning, she went over the evidence
Becca had collected from the shore of Lake Loyal. She'd
assigned the task to her rookie officer in the interest of
being thorough, not because she'd held out much hope
the killer dropped a calling card. Now going over the list,
she had even less hope.

A faded soda can, a tissue, a shot gun shell, and a
collection of Old Milwaukee beer bottles that had probably scattered the lakeshore since Val was a girl. Was it
too much to ask for cigarette butts carrying the DNA of
Kelly's murderer?

She put in a call to the state crime lab, requesting they
expedite analysis of the items, then had a long telecon-
ference with Monica Forbes in the DA's office about the

original homicide, now officially a Jane Doe, and Kelly's most recent death.

It was late by the time she loaded two boxes of files from the original case in the trunk of her unmarked Crown Vic. Her watch read close to midnight by the time she made it home.

The windows were dark, not even the Christmas lights twinkling, when she pulled into the garage next to the bright green Ford Focus. When Grace had turned sixteen last summer, she'd adopted the tiny vehicle as her car, since the PD provided one for Val, and she was pretty self-sufficient, driving herself where she needed to go. But Val wasn't ready to give up eating dinner together and tucking her niece in.

Tonight she'd missed both.

She climbed out, and after closing the door behind her as quietly as possible, circled to the trunk. It took three tries before she could get her numb fingers to hold onto the handle of the first Jane Doe file box. Using her thigh to help support the weight, she managed to wrestle it through the door and reach the kitchen table. The second box would have to wait.

She'd started a pot of coffee and spread the first folder open on the table when she heard the shuffle of slippers descend the stairs.

Tucking her hand under the table, she turned a smile on Grace. "Sorry to wake you."

"I was awake."

"This late? Physics get the better of you?"

"Finished before the six o'clock news."

She supposed her television viewing choice explained the teenager 's inability to sleep. Even though she'd told her niece the situation over the phone, seeing the news report, complete with the kind of sensationalism that sold advertising spots, had obviously upset her. "I wish you hadn't watched."

Grace padded to the table. In shapeless blue plaid flannel and her long blond hair in a braid, she looked every bit as young as she'd been when she came to live with Val three years ago, at the age of thirteen. But the girl had always understood things way beyond her years, and as much baby fat as still rounded her features, her gray eyes felt much older.

She slid into a chair. "Can I help?"

Val flipped the file folder closed. "Not a good idea."

"You can't protect me forever, Aunt Val."

"Not forever maybe, but I can tonight."

"Was he innocent after all?"

Val shook her head. "We made a mistake about the victim's identity. That doesn't mean he's innocent."

"But you can't keep him in prison if he was convicted for killing someone he didn't kill."

Sometimes she wished Grace wasn't such a star student. "We'll find out who she was."

"How?"

"Don't know yet, but I'll figure it out. Did you feed the horses?"

She tilted her chin down, shooting Val a classic under the brow stare. "I always feed the horses."

"Yes, you do." Grace was more responsible than any teen should be, and although that fact made Val proud, it also worried her at times. "Feeding time is going to feel extra early tomorrow, if you don't get back to bed."

"I want to help you."

"You can't help with this, sweetie."

"Can't I look through transcripts or interviews? I don't have to look at the gross stuff."

Val looked at the files on the table, dozens more in the boxes. She hated the thought of Grace being tangled up in any of this ugliness, but maybe she could find some relatively innocuous evidence for her to review. Her only other option was to haul this stuff into her office and shut the door, but since she couldn't grip the box well enough to carry it up the stairs, that clearly wasn't going to happen.

She shifted through the folders, finally plucked one containing interviews that shouldn't be too upsetting, and slid it to Grace. "I'll let you help, but only if you sleep in tomorrow and let me feed."

"You don't have—"

"I want to. And I have to get up early anyway. You help me, I help you. Deal?"

"Deal."

She took her hand off the folder. "If there's anything in there you have questions about, let me know. Anything."

She shot Val a grin. "Whatever you say, Chief."

They worked for two hours, reading interviews, looking for leads that hadn't been followed, combing forensic reports. Finally Grace couldn't hide her yawns, gave in to Val's badgering and went to bed.

Val brewed another pot of coffee and took yet another look over files that she'd memorized the first time, searching for answers she knew weren't there. Thoughts of her conversation with David Lund flitted around the corners of her mind.

He'd been defensive when she first approached him, much like he'd been the first time he'd topped her suspect list. But while they talked, she'd sensed a change. A cautious opening she hadn't expected, a willingness to help.

She'd sent Pete to his house to dust for prints and take a look around. Reportedly Lund had cooperated, although the search had turned up no prints beyond his own and nothing suspicious in the house.

She had to admit, she was relieved.

Val liked to tell herself that she felt sorry for the guy, for the hell she'd put him through in the investigation of Kelly's first death. But that wasn't all of what she felt for David Lund. The rest, she couldn't let herself think about.

Today, he'd tried to make her back off with his reference to watching the Playboy Channel, but she figured that alibi was probably true. Lake Loyal was a small town. If he'd gone on a date since Kelly's death, she probably would have heard about it.

She had to wonder if he was aware of her lack of dating, too.

Stupid.

She shook her head, trying to banish those thoughts. She had a homicide to deal with, maybe two. She had a niece and four horses to provide for and Christmas coming up fast. Not to mention her other problems.

But among all these concerns, only one had a window that would slam shut in less than forty-eight hours.

She opened a file holding crime scene photos and scanned them one by one. Pictures of charred bone, the rusty old barrel normally used to burn garbage, the dairy farm just down the road from Val's little horse stable.

She flipped to the images of the house where Kelly Lund had grown up. The two-story white clapboard structure was normal enough for this area. Only the locks on the outsides of the bedroom doors and the rings embedded in basement concrete suggested Kelly's upbringing was a bit different from most farm girls.

When her eyes finally refused to stay open, she folded her arms on the table top and laid her head down as she'd done more than once while working an urgent case.

Though none had been as urgent as this.

Dawn came early and without her getting more than two hours sleep. Her hand was worse, her fingers difficult to move as well as numb, the weakness stealing up her arm. To improve, she needed rest and time and luck, all of which were out of her grasp at the moment.

Soft nickers greeted her when she opened the barn door. Breathing in the scents of wood shavings, hay and the warm smell of horse, she doled out scoops of rolled oats and flakes of alfalfa, then leaned against a stall wall for a moment and listened to the rhythmic grinding of equine teeth.

Her life had changed when she'd taken on Grace and her horses, but it wasn't a change she'd ever regretted. Even now, as lonely as she occasionally felt, she knew she could always get strength from her niece, these beautiful animals, and the job.

The three things that made her who she was.

She reached through the stall bars and scratched the forehead of a mare named Bo, then closed up the barn, drove to the cemetery in darkness and watched the sun rise while the backhoe operator got his machine into position.

Shadows stretched from gravestones, darkening the light blanket of snow. Her breath fogged in the air. The backhoe bit into the ground, straining to break through frost that had claimed the sod and first few inches of soil.

It was taking too long.

Everything was taking too long.

She shrugged her wool coat tighter around her neck and looked out past the growling machine. Sunrise Ridge cemetery was perched on the slope of one of the bluffs overlooking Lake Loyal, and from here she could see the pink light of dawn glowing off the partially frozen water and snow-dusted town huddled on its banks.

When she'd first gotten the job here, she'd thought the place charming, if a little backward at times. Since then it had grown to be her home, the residents practical and predictable and friendly more often than not. Just what she'd been looking for when she'd moved north after her sister had died from cancer.

A place that would be safe for raising Melissa's daughter.

And as she stared down at the square little buildings lining Walnut Street, all decked out in wreaths and bows and looking like a painting of the good old days, she couldn't dismiss the feeling that everything she loved about this town was about to be ripped apart unless she could find a way to stop it.

The scrape of steel on concrete brought her attention back to the grave.

Most people are familiar with the idea that bodies are buried at least six feet under, yet that measurement didn't account for the concrete vault surrounding the casket. The lid of that vault was only a couple of feet below the sod, and after a couple of scrapes with the backhoe and a few more with shovels, the men were ready to lift the vault's lid.

A car door slammed.

She spun around to see Jeffrey Schneider winding toward her through the headstones, frost-stiffened grass and patches of snow crackling under his shoes. Close to seventy, the retired chief of police was still a fit and good-looking man. His hair was a lot more salt than pepper, but he had a sparkle in his hazel eyes when he was happy and enough energy to put younger men to shame.

"Jeff. Am I glad to see you." She wasn't sure what that said about her ability to lead the department on her own, but it was the truth.

"You should have called me."

She should have known that would be the first thing he fired her way. "I assume you've talked to Olson."

"He was concerned."

"He told you about his suggestion?"

"He was just trying to protect you."

"Protect me?" She could buy that Olson wanted to protect the people of Lake Loyal, wanting to protect her was a stretch.

He let out a long sigh, as if what came next was going to hurt him. "You've got to know as soon as Hess's attorney files her motion, someone from her firm will start working on a lawsuit. There's going to be an investigation, into the case, into you."

Even though she was trying not to contemplate that far ahead, she knew he was right. No doubt raptors of all kinds were already starting to circle. And the fact that she was Lake Loyal's first female police chief only made her easier prey. "Politics happen, Jeff. I can't think about that now."

His face reddened and he shook his head as if disgusted with her. "You can't ignore it either. You've got to play your hand close to the vest."

"I'm not going to say a word about Olson's suggestion, if that's what you're worried about."

"I'm not."

"Then what?"

He shifted his gaze away, watching as the casket rose from the vault. "I heard David Lund was the one to drag in the body."

"Olson told you that, too?"

He shook his head. "Oneida."

That sounded about right. Oneida Perkins was a great dispatcher and office manager, but she was yet another one who believed Schneider was still chief.

"Are you looking at him again?"

"Of course."

He gave her a hard look, as if sensing her hesitation. "He was here two years ago. He's here now. Seems like a good bet."

She didn't want to talk about it. She was the chief of police now, not Schneider, a fact he seemed to forget as easily as the rest of the town.

"Did Harlan confirm the body is Kelly?"

She nodded. "I talked to him last night. Fingerprints matched."

"Do you have a time of death?"

"Her body is partially frozen, so Harlan hasn't been able to complete the autopsy. But we know she wasn't spotted during the midnight patrol, and she was discovered at the two p.m. patrol."

"So all you know for certain is that she entered the lake sometime between afternoon patrols."

"Right. We're canvassing for people who might have walked through the park during the day, but she wasn't visible from the playground, so I'm not hopeful."

"Does David Lund have an alibi for those twenty-four hours?"

She blew out a breath of frustration. "Not for the entire time, no."

"There you go. You have your vic and you have your killer."

It wasn't quite that simple, but since her former chief probably wouldn't appreciate her pointing that out, she changed the subject. "I still have to figure out who this is." She nodded toward the grave.

"Oh, I might be able to help there."

"How?"

"I've lived here all my life. I know a lot of people, and I was once married to one of Kelly's aunts."

Now that he mentioned it, she did remember he had a tie to the family. Of course, once they'd determined Kelly was the only female still alive, it hadn't mattered. They'd believed they'd identified their victim.

Now she'd like to know more. "What happened, if you don't mind my asking?"

"We turned twenty-five, and the magic was gone."

"Twenty-five, huh?"

"About a year after I became a cop."

The stories of cops getting divorced over the demands of the job were so common, she didn't need to ask details. She'd been engaged, but never actually reached the altar, though her romance had dissolved for a much different reason.

She rubbed the fingers of her right hand with her left. The numbness had reached her wrist now, and although she could still move her fingers, it was growing more and more difficult. She could only hope the problem stopped there.

"So which of Kelly's aunts did you marry?"

"Elizabeth."

Val called up the name on her mental list. "Died in a car wreck, right?"

"That was years after our divorce. Kelly's mother told me the news. I haven't kept in touch with the family, but I remember some of them. I can call around, see what I find."

She felt like an idiot.

She was being too sensitive to Olson's deference to the chief. Oneida's, too. With only forty-eight hours, she didn't have time for ego. She couldn't allow hers to get in the way. "I appreciate the help, Jeff."

"Happy to give it. To tell the truth, I'm a little sick of retirement. Never thought playing cards would get old, but I guess you live and learn." He reached out a hand and patted her shoulder. "Don't worry. We'll figure it out."

She had to smile at the we. They only needed Olson here, and it would be just like old times. "I hope you're right."

"Me, too." His smile faded before hers. "If we don't come up with anything, and Dixon Hess gets out …" He shook his head. "After seeing what he did to that girl in Nebraska, I doubt a lawsuit will be enough to satisfy him."

Chapter
Five

By the time Val reached the morgue, the numbness in her hand had inched to her elbow, and the sun was already in the western sky. She was late, she was cold, and she was teetering closer and closer to the edge of desperation.

Monica Forbes stood beside the ridiculous old hearse Harlan had bought from a local funeral home for his personal vehicle, her arms wrapped around herself as tightly as the scarf wrapped around her head.

Slipping into an empty space, Val unlocked the passenger door for the assistant district attorney.

Monica slipped into the seat, closed the door, and shivered. "I know this is going to feel warm by the time we get to January, but I'm freezing."

"You should have waited inside."

"Can't stand the smell. Besides, I wanted a chance to talk to you … unfortunately *not* about the sex I had last night. Have you ever used a rabbit vibrator?"

Monica had been discovering the overabundant joys of sex since she'd met a man three months ago, a guy she was now engaged to marry. Val used to tease her about it, at first, now Monica tried to beat her to the punch and brought up some new experience every time they talked. "What happened?"

"Well, it's ribbed and—"

"With the case, Monica."

She shot Val a fleeting grin, then became dead serious. "Tamara Wade filed a habeas corpus motion on Hess's behalf at three o'clock yesterday."

"That's less than an hour after we found the body."

"Makes you wonder, right? I mean, did she have a draft ready to go? Was she just waiting for Kelly Lund's body to be pulled from the lake? Maybe you should find out if she has an alibi." Monica arched an over-plucked eyebrow.

Of course, they didn't yet know if Kelly's death was homicide. It could always be suicide or even a drunken accident. At least she could hope.

The thought of having two murder investigations on her hands made Val's head spin. It wasn't that she doubted her department. Lake Loyal had a damn good PD, and she'd worked her ass off to make sure it had only gotten better in the past six months. But Lake Loyal was a small town. Her department was set up to enforce traffic laws, defuse domestics and crack down on drunk drivers, not investigate multiple homicides.

Val didn't have a clue how she was going to come up with the manpower. She'd have to go to the county for help.

"You have Jane Doe?" Monica glanced into the car, the slight flinch on her face suggesting she was hoping not to see the bones loose on the back seat.

"She's already in the morgue."

"Then I'm sure Harlan has identified her and we can just wrap this up." Monica shot her a grin. "I'm an optimist."

"At least one of us is."

The sunny expression slipped from Monica's face. "I also wanted to warn you that I've heard rumblings."

"Let me guess. Lawsuit? Investigation?"

"Everyone expects Hess to sue. There's a cap as to what he can get from the state, but I don't think anyone's worried about the money. Not really."

"They want someone to blame."

"And you and I are in their crosshairs."

Val thought of Chief Schneider's warning. That's what it came down to. Make sure Hess stayed in prison or prepare for the avalanche of blame that would bury not only her, but Monica, too.

Not to mention what Hess would do once he was free.

"Let's see what Harlan can tell us," Val said.

In her career as a cop, Val had spent more time in a morgue than she'd ever dreamed possible, and yet she still felt that cold shiver as soon as she stepped foot inside.

Monica was right. It was the smell.

There weren't many bodies in and out of the little county morgue, not like the endless parade in Chicago, but the place still held that fleshy, slightly sweet odor that no disinfectant or air freshener could mask.

Once she'd made the mistake of wearing her street clothes to the autopsy of a man whose body had been found by a deer hunter in the forest preserve. She'd never liked the outfit much, so it wasn't a big loss, but her date she'd met for dinner after hadn't been amused.

Come to think of it, *he* wasn't much of a loss either.

Today was different though. In addition to that dead smell, there was another she knew equally well. The scent of burned bone had hung in her hair and coated her skin for weeks leading up to Dixon Hess's arrest.

Monica hovering in the hall behind her, Val stepped around the scale built into the floor for weighing bodies at check in and ducked her head into the small evidence room off to the right. "Hello?"

"In here, sweet knees." A gruff voice said from down the hall.

Harlan Runk was one of the most grizzled old coots Val had run across in Wisconsin, and that was saying something. Even the times she'd seen him in court dressed in suit and tie, he still managed to look like he'd just come in from an extended fishing trip or deer hunting excursion with the boys. His gray hair was rumpled, a two-day shadow of salt-and-pepper stubble covered scarred cheeks. Even his eyebrows resembled a backwoods thicket.

But despite his appearance and propensity for using nicknames and veiled come-ons that would set even an anti-feminist's teeth on edge, he'd always been competent and eager to help in any way he could.

With Val, that counted for a lot.

She found him in the autopsy room, hunched over a to-go container, eating what looked like spaghetti in a lumpy tomato sauce or ... something.

He glanced up, a splotch of red dotting his silver stubbled chin. "Decided to go ahead and eat. Thought you were going to be here before lunch."

"Sorry. I was held up."

He squinted past her, spotting Monica. "And how do, counselor? Haven't seen you down here very often."

"Hello, Mr. Runk."

"So formal? Even when I'm not in the witness box?"

"I like to keep things professional."

Val stifled a smile. Obviously Monica didn't quite know how to deal with Harlan. Not surprising. Most women teetered on the edge between squicked out and patronizing.

He focused on her, tilting his head to one side like a dog trying to make sense of human language. "I heard you're being investigated."

"Not yet, Harlan. Not yet."

"Not fair, you ask me. That Jane Doe sure didn't hack herself to pieces, jump in that barrel, douse herself with gasoline, and light the match."

Val eyed the collection of charred bones already laid out on the stainless steel gurney. "Have you had a chance to examine her?"

"Little bit. Not sure what you think we're going to find that we didn't before."

"Unfortunately, I don't either. But I live in hope."

Monica the optimist gave a supportive nod.

He shoveled a few more bites into his mouth, leaving his lips tinged red with sauce, then tossed the Styrofoam in the trash and sidled up to the gurney of bones. With gloved hands, he picked up each, in turn, making grunting sounds in the back of his throat.

Monica was the first to speak. "What do you see?"

"Some bones. Well done."

She rolled her eyes. "Anything that could help us identify her or lead to her killer?"

"No teeth, no flesh, most of these bones aren't even in one piece, dried out and shattered from the heat." He glanced over a copy of his original autopsy report, then peered up at Val. "I don't know what to say, honey bun. Don't see anything to change or anything to add. Maybe you need to show these to an expert on fire deaths, like a forensic anthropologist. Maybe call down to Madison."

"It's a good idea, but I'm afraid I'm short on time." Only one day left, twenty-four hours, and she had nothing more than she'd had in the original investigation. She hoped Schneider and Olson had found a lead in their calls to Kelly's family members.

"How about the body you took fingerprints from yesterday? Have you gotten a chance to examine her?" There was no telling how Kelly factored in to Jane Doe's death, or if she did at all, but Val needed anything she could get.

"Still frozen as a Thanksgiving turkey. Well maybe not quite, but it takes a while, you know. I took some x-rays and did the external exam. I think I might have something you'll want to see."

The external part of an autopsy was always the most interesting to Val, since in her experience, most evidence in a homicide tended to be found on the outside of the body. And although she would never admit it to anyone, whenever the cutting began, she was never sure if she was going to be sick or simply faint. Between that and severe time constraints, she was relieved the internal exam would wait for another day.

"I'll get her out of the cooler." Harlan padded across the small room, the soles of his Keds squeaking on the tile.

Val followed, but when he pulled open the door, she was sorry she had. Two sheet-covered gurneys and miscellaneous paper grocery bags and black evidence bags filled nearly half of the tiny space. Cold sweetness engulfed her in a wave. Her stomach gave a shudder.

Monica lagged behind, looking as if she might have to make a run for the restroom at any moment.

"Sorry about the stink. One of these was a lady who lived alone. She wasn't found until the neighbor heard the dog yelping. A week after the lady died, and the poor thing finally ran out of food." He pushed his way between the gurneys and grabbed the one near the wall, chuckling to himself. "Funny thing. Neighbor lived next to her twenty years, yet couldn't identify her. Not without her face."

Monica turned a deeper shade of green.

Even Val was wishing she'd stayed back in the autopsy theater. Or better yet, outside in the car. "Thanks for sharing that image, Harlan."

"I'm sure you saw worse things in Chicago."

"That's why I moved here."

"Once we're done, I'll put the old girl in the freezer, solid her up a little and clear the air in here." He wheeled out his chosen body and closed the door behind him, cutting off the stench.

Or most of it.

Val pushed the image of pets eating faces to the back of her mind and focused on the shape under the autopsy sheet.

Harlan positioned the gurney in front of the oblong stainless steel sink. In Chicago, the morgue had been huge with many people working under the medical examiner. But in a small county like this one, the coroner was an elected position, and often didn't even have a medical degree.

Harlan was an actual forensic pathologist, but he had only a handful of people in his entire department and space to perform one autopsy at a time. It was a good thing the body count was low. Three bodies in the morgue, counting Jane Doe's bone fragments, made for a huge back up.

He clipped x-rays to the lighted board. "My daughter's son broke an arm, and the hospital had x-rays right there on the computer screen. Of course with all the budget cuts around here, I'll be dead before we get more than this damn light box."

Val squinted at the gray outlines of bones. "Is anything broken?"

"Nope."

"Find any fibers? Material under her nails?"

Pete Olson had bagged her hands at the scene, and they'd wrapped her in a sheet before loading her into the ambulance to preserve any trace evidence. Of course, since she had been in the lake, the odds of them finding anything useful were slim.

"Fingernails looked clean, but I'll send samples of everything to the crime lab. In fact, I could use a gofer."

Wisconsin had three crime labs, the closest in Madison. But as with everything else, budgets were tight. It was hard to say how large a back log they were dealing with or just when Val might see reports on what they found.

"I'll send my newest officer. As long as you promise not to scare her away."

"Oh, I'd never do that, sugar lips."

"Seriously, be polite."

He held up a hand. "I swear."

She focused back on the gurney. "You have photos?"

"Yep. But this you should see in person." He removed the evidence sheet, uncovering Kelly's head and naked shoulders. Like at the lake, her skin was the color of freezer burned chicken, her once blue eyes colorless.

"Hold on." Harlan pulled on a new pair of gloves and gently probed along the top of her cheekbone with an index finger. Grunting as if in answer to a question posed by his own thoughts, he picked up a syringe from the tray of instruments. "Still frozen, but she's thawed enough now to take fluid. This'll take just a sec."

Realizing what he was about to do, Val glanced toward the ceiling.

"What you looking at? You got to see this."

Swallowing into a tight throat, she forced her eyes to return to Kelly's face.

Harlan pushed the upper and lower lids of one eye back to more clearly reveal a dull, ghostly gray eye. He held the syringe in his other hand, the needle poised only centimeters away. "See that?"

She leaned forward. "See what?"

"Subconjunctival hemorrhage. The capillaries in the eyes. They're broken."

"A sign of strangulation."

"Could be. Likely just from struggling to breathe before she drowned. No bruising at the throat. No sign of any other injuries. Maybe I'll find more when I cut her open." Before she could look away, he plunged the needle into Kelly's eye and drew fluid into the syringe. "Yup, looks like she's thawing nicely."

Val's face felt hot, her head light. She breathed through her mouth to keep the smells from adding to her misery.

On television, cops were so tough, never flinching at the sights and smells of death and the more than distasteful procedures in the morgue. She'd known real cops like that, but she'd never been one of them. She'd always had to work hard just to keep it together.

"Uh, let me know what you find." Monica bolted out of the autopsy suite. The bathroom door down the hall slammed shut.

Val hoped she wouldn't have to join her. "The eyes, is that what you wanted me to see, Harlan?"

Having noted and logged his sample, Harlan returned to the gurney. He peeled back the sheet, exposing Kelly's bare body. "There's also this."

He moved his hand over her belly and pointed to the thin, red line stretching like a smile above Kelly's trimmed strip of pubic hair.

"Oh my God," Val heard herself say. "She had a C-section."

Harlan nodded. "Looks like our girl here was somebody's mommy."

Chapter
Six

"You have to, Val." Monica stared her down over evidence files that had failed to yield anything they hadn't seen before.

Val stifled a yawn. Except for a short dinner break, she and Monica had been holed up in her office since leaving the morgue, and in all those hours, they'd gotten exactly nowhere on their quest to identify Jane Doe and tie her death to Hess. A glance at her watch showed almost three in the morning.

Jeff Schneider, with Olson's help, had tracked down a male cousin on Kelly's mother's side who'd supplied them with a list of family members. Unfortunately they'd come up with the same result as Val had the first time. The women who would have shared mito DNA with Kelly had been dead and buried for years. The cousin had even supplied lists of three cemeteries where the past few generations were buried, the one on Sunrise Ridge and two in northern Illinois. The rest of her relations were either not part of her maternal line or male, facts which struck them from contention.

In addition to the Jane Doe case, she'd been trying to juggle the investigation into Kelly's death. She'd arranged for two SCUBA divers with the sheriff's department to check the area where Kelly was found, but there was no sign of a baby. If the child wasn't with Kelly when she died, it was alone, someone was watching it, or the killer had taken it. They needed to find that baby. Just one more urgent thing to add to the list.

And now Monica had gotten the idea into her head that Val should make one last ditch effort to confront Hess before he became a free man.

"Hess's hearing is on the afternoon docket, so he'll be brought down to the jail tomorrow morning." Monica took a sip of coffee, shooting Val a strong stare over the rim of her mug.

"What are you hoping to get from this? He's not going to confess."

"Don't sell yourself short." She raised her eyebrows and nodded in an attempt at encouragement. "If not a confession, maybe something just as good. A slip up. A detail we missed. It doesn't have to be gift wrapped, just something we can use to arrest him before he walks out the door."

Val wanted to buy into Monica's seemingly endless optimism, but the fact was, she knew Hess much better than the DA did. "I've talked to him before, remember? Hess doesn't slip up, and he only hands out details that help him."

"So use the baby."

Val brought her own cup to her lips. She couldn't even taste the coffee, it was so weak, but it gave her a chance to stall a beat, to think.

"Come on, Val. Harlan said the caesarean scar is less than a year old. The baby fits the timeline." Monica counted off points on her fingers. "Kelly gets pregnant, then disappears. We find Jane Doe and believe she's Kelly. But even though Kelly's alive, she doesn't come forward. Not even through a sensational trial. Why?"

She could see where Monica was heading. "Kelly was glad Hess was arrested. She left because she was afraid of him."

Monica gave an enthusiastic nod. "Maybe because the baby is Hess's."

"Or maybe it's not."

"Either way, Kelly chose to let the world believe she was dead so that Hess would go to prison. He has to have some kind of reaction to that."

Val set her cup on the desk. "It is something we didn't know before."

Monica perched on the edge of her chair. "You think it might work? Shock him into saying something he normally wouldn't?"

"I doubt it."

"But you'll give it a shot?"

Val checked her watch again. She had only a few hours to figure out how she would approach Hess, and time relentlessly ticked away. "I guess I'll have to."

In a room full of average men, Dixon Hess would win a prize for being the most average.

His light brown hair was short, but not too short. His clean-shaven face was pleasant at first glance, but not too pleasant. He was already dressed for court, wearing a suit, his shirt a crisp white, his tie disarming pink. To a casual observer, he probably looked like any upstanding guy on his way to any office job in any city across the country. In a word, generic.

But only if they weren't close enough to see his eyes.

Ice blue. Hard. So sharp, Val could feel them cut.

He sat next to his lawyer, a stylish-on-a-budget public defender named Tamara Wade. But though she was leaning close, talking in his ear, he didn't seem to be listening.

All of his attention was focused on Val.

She nodded to the two deputies in the room, took her chair, and plunked the heavy file she was carrying on the table top. She would have preferred a room with no table, leaving Hess more exposed so she could better read his body language, but at short notice, this small conference room was all she could get.

At least the table would also hide her vulnerabilities from him.

"Chief Valerie Ryker," he said, slowly running his tongue over her name. "Congratulations on the new title."

"Thank you."

"Aren't you going to congratulate me on my freedom?"

She forced her lips into a smile but didn't say a word. Often the simple act of saying nothing was a more effective interview technique than all the words in the dictionary. Silence increased the pressure, made the subject eager to fill the void, to explain away his guilt.

Val wasn't sure that was going to work with Hess.

He seemed too relaxed, almost at ease, leaning against the back of his chair as if slightly bored. Where people under stress carried a smell about them, a cross between sweat and a visceral edge of fear, the only scent she could detect was Tamara's perfume.

If there was anyone in this room feeling pressure, it was Tamara. Or Val herself.

She held his gaze and waited, seconds feeling like minutes, but nothing seemed to change. Voices rumbled out in the hall. One of the bailiffs shifted his shoes on the floor, the keys in his belt jingling.

"Police Chief Ryker?" The lawyer broke the standoff, addressing the camera looking down at them from the corner. "I've advised my client not to talk to you. In fact, I am entirely opposed to this meeting."

"Noted," Val responded to Tamara, but she kept her eyes on Hess. "If you have nothing to hide, why be afraid to talk to me?"

"Actually I'm more in the mood to listen."

"Fine." She flipped open the folder, although there wasn't a word or image in it that she didn't know in excruciating detail. "We have uncovered a number of additional facts since this case was prosecuted."

"Is this a preview of what you'll be presenting at the hearing?" Tamara asked.

"That depends." Val gave a non-committal tilt of her head. Unless Hess slipped up, the prosecution wouldn't have anything to present.

"Depends on what?" the lawyer asked.

"On what your client has to say."

"Don't tell me. The person you say I killed wasn't Kelly Lund after all?"

Tamara shot Hess a nervous glance. "He's doing you a favor by listening to you. He's not answering questions."

"Fine."

"So what are your issues?"

The way she phrased it, you'd think Val was coming to her for counseling, not interviewing her client.

Val had been right. Questioning Hess had been a bad idea. It would have been one thing if she was talking to him alone. Then she might be able to use the baby to goad him into slipping up. Maybe. But Tamara Wade was no dummy. The more Val talked, the more likely the lawyer was to notice that she had little new information that pertained to the Jane Doe murder and nothing that implicated her client.

Best to keep the exchange short and shocking. "The most interesting thing we've found was at Kelly's autopsy."

"You're not planning to accuse me of her murder, are you? Because I have a pretty convincing alibi."

"No, I don't think you killed Kelly."

"Finally. Guess a guy's got to be locked in prison before you believe him."

"But we did find that during the time she was gone …" Val paused for a beat. "… Kelly gave birth."

"A child?" Tamara's voice spiked. She turned wide eyes on her client.

Hess's sharp eyes remained steady, his face a mask of calm. "Where is the baby?"

"I thought you were in the mood to listen, not ask or answer questions."

"My mood has changed."

Tamara Wade held up her hand. "I have to advise—"

"Shut it," Hess said.

The defense lawyer visibly cringed.

Hess's ice pick eyes drilled into Val. "Where is he?"

"He?" At no time had she referred to the baby as he.

"The child."

"How do you know the child is a boy?"

"You don't know where he is, do you? You don't have a clue."

Of course, she didn't, not that she hadn't tried. Not that she wouldn't keep trying. But at this point, she hadn't even found the hospital where Kelly had given birth, provided it was in a hospital at all. "We're following up some leads."

"Games. That's what this is all about, isn't it? It's a game to you. Trying to get me to talk, get me to tell you something you don't know, because you've hit a dead end."

"I don't play games." Sure it was a lie. But that was part of the game.

A smile curled the corners of his lips, but his eyes remained cold. "Neither do I. That's one of the things I learned in Waupun. Life is too short. I play for keeps."

"How do you know about the baby?"

"That's easy. Kelly told me. We were both very happy about the news."

In preparation for the interview, Val had checked a list of his prison visitors. Beyond his lawyer, Hess hadn't had any. "When did she tell you?"

"The day she disappeared."

"How far along was she?"

"A couple of weeks."

"That's awfully early for her to know the gender. How do you know it's a boy?"

He shrugged a shoulder. "I always wanted a son."

Right. Val had an idea where the news might have come from. She stole a glance Tamara's way. "Who told you about the baby, Tamara?"

The attorney's face grew pale. "Excuse me?"

"You were his only visitor. I checked the records."

She shook her head, strawberry blond bob swinging like a shampoo commercial. "He received mail, too."

"And it's monitored. I checked. No, the news had to come from you."

"Whatever I talked about with my client is protected."

Hess's chuckle grated on Val's nerves.

The lawyer might not have to spill her secrets, but that didn't mean Val couldn't follow up. Unfortunately failing to admit how he knew the baby's gender wasn't a chargeable offense. "So the baby is yours, Hess? You know that for certain?"

"Of course, the baby is mine."

"If Kelly told you she was pregnant, and you were both so happy, why didn't she come forward when you were arrested for her murder? Why would she let you go to prison?"

"Why does a woman do anything, Chief? I think you can probably answer that better than I can."

"You must have been very angry when you found out she was alive."

Another hint of a chilling smile. "I found out when my lawyer told me. And unfortunately, by then Kelly was already dead."

"Why didn't you say anything at your trial?"

"Haven't you been listening? I didn't know she was alive."

"But you knew the woman in that barrel wasn't Kelly. Who was she?"

He blew a derisive laugh through his nose. "Nice try, Chief Valerie. But you said you didn't play games."

"Not a game. A sincere question."

"Then I'll give you a sincere answer, and I'll make it as clear as I can." This time he held up a silencing hand even before Tamara could open her mouth. "I did not kill that woman you found. I have no idea who killed her or who she was. You were the one who said it was Kelly, and as far as I knew, that could have been true. But I didn't kill her. I was framed for that murder."

"Listen, I know Kelly's family wasn't as apple pie as they've been made out to be. I've seen the house, the locks on the outside of the bedroom doors. I'm sure they weren't the easiest people to deal with."

"You have no idea."

"I'm sure you had good reason."

Hess gave a dramatic yawn. "I've had enough of answering your questions, Valerie. I have a question for you."

Val set her jaw. "Ask away."

"Do you believe in justice?"

She didn't hesitate. "Yes."

For the first time since Val had entered the room, he spared a glance at his attorney. "See? That wasn't so hard. Some people can answer a simple question."

Tamara didn't say a word or make a movement, but Val swore she could see the woman withdraw like a turtle retreating into her shell at his threat.

"Is that why you killed the woman at the Meinholz farm and burned her body? Justice? Did Kelly's father do something to you?"

He shook his head, slowly, deliberately. "Prison is a bad place to be, Chief Val. You have no idea how much noise and smell a shithole full of men can produce. Not to mention the never ending mystery over whether your cellie is more interested in fucking or killing you. But that isn't the worst part. Do you know what is?"

Val didn't answer.

"The worst part is losing what was mine. That's what it all comes down to, isn't it? You want to really hurt a man, you take away what he loves the most. You take away what's *his*."

"What did you lose, Hess?"

"My son. My freedom. My reputation."

Despite her effort to control her response, Val let out a disbelieving huff on that last one.

Hess raised his brows. "You don't think my reputation is important to me?"

"Maybe I should call down to Omaha and see what the police there think."

"Maybe you should. And if you really do believe in justice, and you look hard enough at the evidence in

55

that case—not what the cops made up—you'll see it all doesn't tie together like you want it to."

He leaned toward Tamara, taking a peek at her watch. "Now we have a hearing to get ready for. If you want to chat again, I'll see you on the outside."

Chapter
Seven

Val squinted through the salt-spotted windshield at the county courthouse. She wasn't sure how long a habeas corpus hearing and press conference would take, but as the sun dipped closer to the horizon and shadows deepened on the fresh snow, she had the feeling it wasn't merely night that was creeping over her little town.

"You okay, Chief?"

At the sound of Becca's voice, Val started. After her disastrous interview with Hess, culminating in his do-you-believe-in-justice threat and reference to the Omaha case, she'd returned to Lake Loyal and started going through the reports she'd had sent up from Nebraska for her original investigation. Since Hess had been acquitted in the Omaha murder, Monica hadn't been able to use any of it at trial, but the evidence in that case had given Val insight into the kind of man she was dealing with. Now she realized the file was woefully incomplete.

If there was something specific about that case Hess was referring to, she couldn't see it. So she'd called the Omaha PD and requested further reports, and then unable to sit around and wait for Armageddon, she'd decided to drive to the courthouse and watch it begin. Her eager rookie officer had talked her way into driving her there.

"I'm fine. Just a little tired," Val said. She turned to face the driver's side of the squad car and noticed Becca eyeing her hand. She stuffed it into her pocket.

"You sure you're okay?"

"Fingers are just stiff. Probably a little arthritis or carpal tunnel or something."

"I have ibuprofen in my bag."

Val waved off the offer. "It's nothing. I just wish they'd hurry up. How long can a habeas corpus hearing take?"

"And a press conference."

Of course. Val wouldn't want to forget the press conference. She could imagine the headlines and front page photos peppering newspapers and local TV across Wisconsin tonight.

INNOCENT MAN FREED AFTER MURDER VICTIM FOUND IN FROZEN LAKE.

Innocent.

She shook her head. If she was really lucky, they'd include a photo of her from the old investigation footage; her blond hair tied back, her uniform making her look severe and more than a little pear shaped. And maybe they'd even point out that this false conviction had landed her the job of police chief, that she'd built her career on the back of this poor, downtrodden, innocent man.

But as bad as all that would be, she had a feeling things were going to get much worse.

"Looks like they're done," Becca said.

Val raised her left hand, shielding her eyes from the glare. Movement shuffled through the glass doors of the squat, brick county building. The media came out first, television cameras looking for the money shot, reporters and local news personalities following, either scribbling notes or fixing makeup and hair, depending on their medium.

County deputies took their spots on either flank of the small crowd of parka-clad curious. Not exactly the size and fervor one would find in Val's native Chicago, but something the area had likely never seen. At least not since Hess's conviction.

Now they had only to wait for the guest of honor.

An uncomfortable shimmer of energy raced along Val's nerves, the kind of feeling she got when things were about to go very wrong. She concentrated on her breathing, in four counts, hold four counts, out four counts, and clasped her hands in her lap. Her numb fingers felt cold to the touch. How could she have forgotten her gloves?

The glass doors opened, two more deputies emerged and then the man himself.

A few people trailed behind, his lawyer, some others, but Val couldn't focus on anyone but Hess. He was dressed the same as he had been this morning, with the addition of a dark gray coat over his suit. He held his head high as he performed his perp walk in reverse. A free man. A proud man.

An innocent man.

Val felt sick to her stomach.

"So what happens now?" Again, Becca's voice gave her a jolt.

"We work to put him back."

"And if we can't?"

"We will."

It occurred to Val that her protégé had no inkling of how comfortably boring small town police work could be. Boredom for which Val had developed a physical longing.

She could hardly remember what it felt like to take a day off, to watch the Packers with a beer in hand, cross country ski through the trails in Devil's Lake State Park, or sleep all day just because she wanted to.

Because she needed to.

At the curb, Hess and Tamara Wade split ways, the lawyer walking a little faster as if eager to get away from him. She climbed into a silver-blue Volvo parked at the curb.

He paused next to a burgundy SUV that had seen better days, but instead of getting in the vehicle, he spun around and stared straight at Val.

"Oh my God," Becca whispered under her breath.

The sharp blue eyes flicked to Becca, taking her in. Then his lips pulled back in a smile, revealing straight white teeth.

Val had an overpowering urge to lean to the side, blocking his view of the young officer.

She'd been stupid to come, stupid to show him how interested she was in noting his every move, really stupid to bring a young woman along, cop or not, that he could notice, fixate on. Hadn't she just been reading about the young woman he'd tortured to death in Nebraska? "Let's get out of here."

Becca shifted into gear.

When they drove past Hess, he was still watching, and Val shot her hardest stare right back. But even after they were safely down the road, her whole body was shaking, and she wondered how soon she'd see Dixon Hess again.

By the time Becca dropped her back at the station and left to enjoy what was left of her day off, Val's blood was buzzing. Hess might have dressed his threat up as a question of justice and a lament about how much he'd lost, but Val recognized it for what it was. She needed to make sure everyone involved with the investigation and trial was informed and protected.

She started with Pete Olson, who had finally gone home to his wife and kids for the first time in days. In true Olson form, he wasn't surprised by the threat, in fact, he said only two words.

"I'm ready."

Monica Forbes was prepared as well. Answering on her cell, the assistant district attorney was almost inaudible over the chimes and beeps in the background.

"Where are you?"

"The local casino. We're staying at the hotel. Might as well take advantage of the slots. And you know hotel sex is always the best."

For Monica, Val was getting the idea that any and all sex was always the best. And she had to admit, the envy she was feeling over her friend's evening had little to do with jamming tokens in slot machines at the casino run by a local Native American tribe.

Next she called Dale Kasdorf, witness to the brawl between Hess and Kelly that left Kelly's blood in his truck right before she disappeared. Val had met Kasdorf her first day on the job when he'd decided to show his appreciation of the Wisconsin open carry law by hanging out in Rossum Park with an AR15 strapped to his back and a Heckler and Koch Mark 23 at his waist.

Once a farm hand at the Meinholz's dairy farm, he now made his living writing a blog and how-to manuals about weapons and survival. He didn't answer the phone—Kasdorf never did—so she had to leave a message.

The last call she made was to David Lund, but he wasn't home either, and apparently he wasn't answering his cell.

After a word with the shift sergeant taking over for Olson, ordering hourly drive-by checks of Kasdorf's and Lund's homes, she left her office and made for the dispatch center, a glorified closet packed to bursting with equipment purchased with Homeland Security money back in 2002. Before that, Val could only guess what the tiny burg of Lake Loyal had gotten by with. Probably a single phone with a pigtailed cord and an old CB radio.

"I thought you were going home."

"Nice to see you, too, Oneida."

The dispatcher, secretary, coffee brewer and cleaning lady, Oneida Perkins ran the station. She'd been Jeff Schneider's right hand woman when he'd been chief, and Val had inherited her bossy mothering. Her unquestioning allegiance still clearly belonged to Schneider.

A large, white woman, Oneida liked to tell anyone who would listen that she had Indian blood running through her veins. Val happened to know her dispatcher had paid a fortune to have her family tree researched, and as far as native roots went, she'd come up empty.

A secret Val would never spill.

Oneida gave her a disapproving frown. "Get out of here. Go home."

The woman was strong on the frown, even when she was happy. And Oneida was never happier than when she was mothering Val. Or bullying her.

Same thing.

"I just have a few things to tie up."

"A few things? It's been days, and you're starting to smell. He's out now, okay? It's done. Time for you to get some rest, come at it fresh tomorrow."

Val slipped her right hand into her coat pocket, not wanting Oneida to see just how badly she needed to take the advice. "I'll leave. I promise. How are things here?"

"Nice and quiet. Just the way we like 'em. Now, go. Get something decent to eat. Get some rest. And for heaven's sake, take a shower. I better not see you again until tomorrow."

A shower would feel good. And food. And sleep. Although the latter might be hard to come by with Hess's threat running through her head.

"I'll schedule a drive-by check or two for you tonight, also," Oneida added, as if reading her mind.

"Thanks," Val told her, and she meant it.

Leaving Oneida humming to herself, Val followed orders and left.

Darkness came early this time of year. And with the long nights came the cold. Her breath fogged the air in front of her. She stuffed her hands deeper into her pockets, still trying to remember where she'd left her gloves.

Her engine rolled over on the first try—thank God for small favors—and she backed out of her space, the power steering squealing in the cold, and pulled onto Branch Street. But instead of turning left on Elmwood, she kept going.

If the television vans had followed him all the way home, they were gone now. She could see that as soon as she made the right onto Bradhearst. She slowed, assessing Hess's building through leafless trees. The apartment she judged to be his was dark, only the soft flicker of television light visible through nicotine-stained blinds.

She scanned the parking lot, looking for the SUV he'd driven from the courthouse, the only vehicle registered in his name.

One pass.

A chill started at the back of her neck and trickled downward.

She turned into the far entrance and wove through the cars, locating spot 217.

No SUV.

No Hess.

She wasn't hungry anymore. Now she felt sick to her stomach.

It had been a good day, the kind of day Tamara Wade had dreamed about when she'd announced to her parents at age fifteen that she wanted to become an attorney.

That same year, she'd also decided she'd be a vegetarian and spend two years in the Peace Corps before going to college.

One out of three wasn't bad.

She drove south on Highway 12 through rolling hills, the lights of Middleton glowing ahead. Norah Jones crooned on her car stereo. The scent of coffee filled the car. When she got home, she'd settle in front of the fireplace, pour a glass of Bordeaux, snuggle her cat and toast to justice.

When she'd taken Dixon Hess's case, she'd been as sure he was guilty as everyone else. She'd worked hard anyway, given him solid legal counsel. No one could have known the authorities had the wrong victim. They had DNA, after all. Juries worshipped DNA. No one could have looked at the facts of the case and come to any conclusion but the one they had.

She couldn't be blamed, but she could claim some credit now. Justice had prevailed. She had prevailed. And she had every right to feel good about it.

She took the off ramp and wound through Middleton's quiet streets. Christmas lights twinkled along rooflines and swags of greenery wrapped light poles. Maybe she wouldn't have Bordeaux. Maybe she'd make it champagne.

The whole thing was funny, really. She'd never liked Dixon Hess. The guy had given her the creeps since the first time she'd seen him. He wasn't bad looking. He could even be charming. But there was something about him that made her uneasy.

She'd obviously listened too much to the prosecution, just as the jury had. If there was one thing she was ashamed of in this case, that was it. She'd believed the smear against her own client and wasn't skeptical enough of the evidence.

That was the only reason she'd agreed to carry those notes to him.

For a moment, a chill stole over her skin despite the fact that the car's heater was turned up to ninety.

But she didn't have to worry. Val Ryker might suspect she'd acted as a messenger for Dixon, but it wasn't as if she'd really done anything wrong, not like Val thought. The notes she'd delivered had nothing to do with the police chief's case against Dixon. It was simply something she could do to make up for the way she'd judged him.

But now that she'd gotten him released, she and Dixon were square. Today, any mistakes she might have made were behind her. And if she was really lucky, she'd never have to see him again.

She swung into the side drive of her apartment building. Approaching the entrance to the underground garage, she used the unit on her dash to raise the door. Pulling into her space, she heaved a satisfied sigh, grabbed her briefcase and climbed out. She was just about to lock the door with her remote, when she spotted movement near the elevator.

Letting the smile she was feeling spread over her lips, she turned to face her neighbor. "Nice night, isn't it?"

No, not her neighbor. "What are you doing here?"

Dixon smiled.

In two seconds he was beside her.

In three, he was smashing her skull into the concrete wall.

Chapter
Eight

After only three or four hours of sleep in the past fifty five, Val would have assumed she'd be snoring before her head hit the pillow.

She would have been right.

What she didn't foresee is jolting awake an hour later.

She stared at the ceiling for another hour, images of burned bones and babies dancing across the slapbrush texture, then she finally kicked back the comforter, climbed out, pulled on a pair of yoga pants and a thick sweater.

Before trading her room for her office, she opened the bedside table and pulled out her weapon. When she'd gotten home, she floated the idea of Grace hopping a bus to somewhere far enough away to be safe. Of course, her niece had refused, citing school and horse chores and the fact that she didn't want to sit in some distant hotel room alone.

All were good points, but that didn't mean Val couldn't overcome them. She just had to figure out the details. A call to Oneida had started the ball rolling on that. And since she couldn't figure out the rest until waking hours for normal people, she might as well get some work done. Her mind wanted to go there anyway.

She settled behind her desk, turned on her computer, and set her gun next to the keyboard. Leaning back in her chair, she closed her eyes.

She didn't want to follow where her thoughts were leading, but she had little choice. The most obvious reason a married woman kept a pregnancy secret from her husband was that the baby wasn't his. And the most obvious reason she would choose to disappear, and stay disappeared, even when the state was in an uproar over her murder, was because she was afraid.

Was Kelly afraid of Hess?

Or was Lund her boogeyman?

In an investigation into a woman's death, the first suspect was always the man she was sleeping with. The odds backed up that assumption, and that was the approach Val had taken from the beginning of this case. She'd scoured every part of David Lund's life, interviewed him several times, put his day-to-day under a magnifying glass. The media had done the same, painting him as Scott Peterson in a cheesehead hat.

Yet all the time, in her gut, Lund hadn't felt right. And after she'd arrested Hess and the media had swung its focus to him, Lund had been left to pick up the shards of his life.

And she'd felt horrible

When Chief Schneider had suggested she take another look at Lund, for the Jane Doe murder and for Kelly Lund, she hadn't wanted to go there. She still didn't, but was it because she knew he was innocent, or she was afraid of what she'd find?

While the computer booted up, she wheeled her chair over to the box of files Grace had carried up for her. Since Lund had been a suspect at the beginning, she had done a good bit of digging into his background. She flipped open his file and laid it on her lap.

The pages staring back at her were interesting in both a bad way and a good. Lund had a juvie record, now sealed. She'd asked him about it originally, but he'd given a vague answer about accidently starting a fire. Then when evidence stacked up against Hess, she'd moved on.

She sure would like to know if there was more to it now.

The good thing was even more compelling. Lund worked as fire inspector as part of his firefighter duties. The position was largely about inspecting buildings to make sure they passed local ordinances, but he'd also had additional training.

She swiveled back to the computer. Hand still in dodgy shape, she manipulated the mouse with her left and tried to ignore the headache and stiffness settling into her head and neck.

Earlier that night, the Omaha PD had sent further information from their failed case against Hess, along with more detailed photos from the scene and the autopsy, ones she hadn't seen before.

She pulled them up on the monitor.

If she thought the first photos she'd examined were gruesome, she was wildly mistaken. Now she could see the precise cuts Hess had made, the layers of skin he'd seared away with the curling iron, the brutal way he'd violated her before dousing her in gasoline and setting her entire body on fire.

Where the Jane Doe's remains were blackened bone, difficult to identify with as human, this woman was clearly a living being. And it was impossible to look at what he'd done to her and not feel overwhelmed with hopelessness for the whole, stinking species.

She called up the autopsy report, each defilement the poor girl had suffered recorded in black and white.

Hess had told her to look hard at the evidence, that she would then see things didn't tie together. But as hard as she'd stared since these files had arrived, she hadn't come to any kind of magical revelation.

Harlan had suggested he send Jane Doe to a forensic anthropologist at the University. A fabulous idea. Surely an expert could see something she couldn't. But that could take weeks or even months, and if there was one thing she didn't have, it was time. She needed to talk to an expert ASAP.

As luck would have it, she had an expert in mind. She just had to convince him to speak to her.

Lund knocked the dusting of morning snow off his boots and stepped into the police department's box-like entrance. Not much bigger than a sally port between doors, the space held a window on one side with a slip through space under the thick glass, like a ticket window. On the other side, he could see part of the tiny dispatch center, essentially a countertop jammed with keyboards and computer monitors.

The Lake Loyal PD was tucked into a corner of the village hall. Even though the department employed fewer than a dozen officers total, the space was so small, it would be overcrowded at half that. Nothing about the place was intimidating, but after teetering on the edge of being locked up for murder every time he'd stepped in the doors, his chest felt a little tight.

"Be right with you, sir."

For a woman who shared a name with one of the Native American tribes in Wisconsin, Oneida didn't look at all Native American. Blond streaked with gray, big boned and more than a little heavy, she was quite the opposite, and was known through town for wearing green and gold to work on Packer game days, and red when the Badgers suited up.

Lund had known Oneida for years, had even gone to school with one of her sisters, but the woman still bunched up her brow every time she saw him, as if she didn't have a clue who he was.

A small thing compared to the indignities he'd suffered in this place.

But this time it was supposed to be different. When Chief Ryker had called, she'd said she needed his opinion as fire inspector. He wasn't sure he believed it, but just the chance of being able to do something beat sitting around staring at a wall.

Oneida bustled to the door and pulled it open. "You're here to see the chief?"

So she remembered him this time. He wasn't sure if that was good or bad. "She asked me to come in."

"She's busy right now. Can you wait?"

"I'll come back another time."

"It won't be long. This interruption … it was unexpected."

If he wasn't mistaken, she seemed flustered. "What's going on?"

"I'm sure she'll be able to see you soon." She scurried around the corner, remarkably fast for a large woman. The lock buzzed, and she pulled the door open. "Follow me. Please."

Her insistence made him nothing but uneasy, nevertheless he stepped inside.

The station was tiny, like the department, like the town. The chief's office was just inside and to the left.

"Follow me." She took off past a collection of four cubicles, their ancient cloth walls having lived through better days. Her shapeless skirt swished with each sway of those serious hips.

Lund moved more slowly, trying to get a glimpse through the glass panel running adjacent to the chief's door. She was inside, as Oneida had said, talking to a man in a suit.

"Are you coming?"

He moved on, following Oneida into a room the size of a closet.

"Have a seat. Cups. Coffee. Help yourself." She whirled and hurried out of the room.

He followed orders, taking his coffee with a dash of powered creamer to soften its on-the-warmer-too-long bite and settling into a plastic chair.

A police break room turned out to look much like any other break room, except for the extra small size. A refrigerator. A microwave that needed cleaning. A soda machine jammed in the corner.

The Wisconsin State Journal stared up at him from the bistro-sized table, Dixon Hess's face above the fold. He dug out the sports page, laid it on top, and started skimming an article about the Packers' playoff chances.

"Sorry about the delay."

Dressed in her uniform and with her blond hair pulled back, Val Ryker looked businesslike, as usual. And yet she gave him a little smile that held, not the suspicion he remembered so well, but something resembling warmth.

What the hell?

Maybe that was what bothered him about her. He could never quite figure out where she was coming from. "You said you wanted my help."

"Yes, I do."

He tossed the paper on the table and stood. "What do you need?"

"Would you like to take your coffee? It's better if we talk in my office."

He followed her and settled into the chair just vacated by her earlier visitor. Although he'd been in the station several times, he'd never been invited into the chief's office, and he had to admit, the space was something of a disappointment. Sure she had plaques and diplomas displayed on the walls, even a framed headline announcing Hess's conviction. Her desk was fairly large and nice compared to the glorified countertop in the dispatch center, but all in all, the décor seemed a bit too bland to give him a sense of the woman at all.

Instead of circling behind the desk, she settled in the chair beside him and angled her body toward him. "Thanks for coming in. I really appreciate it." Another smile.

He wanted to volley with a grin of his own, but he held back. "Sure."

"I have some questions about fire."

"I'm pretty good when it comes to fire."

"I have some pictures to show you. But before we start, I want to clear the air between us."

"Okay."

"If I'm honest with you, will you be honest with me?"

"Depends."

"So it's going to be like that?"

He shrugged a shoulder. "You have your idea of how you want this to go. I'm waiting to see what it is."

"You served time in a juvenile facility as a child."

"About a month."

"What put you there?"

He leaned back in the chair and let out a bitter laugh. "If I'm a suspect again, why not just come out and say so. I thought you wanted to clear the air."

"That's not why I'm asking."

"Oh, really?"

"I need you to consult on a case, and I'd like to fill in that blank before we begin."

"If you don't mind, I don't believe you."

"Your choice. So what put you in juvie?"

He paused for a moment, trying to decide if he'd answer or not. Finally curiosity over what she was getting at won out. "I started a fire. I told you that."

"Did anyone die?"

"No, but an insurance company lost a lot of money. In our society, that's probably worse."

A little smile touched the corners of her mouth, a smile he'd like to believe was real.

"And you served a month for this?" she asked.

"You know I did. And I didn't torture puppies or wet the bed, if those are your follow ups."

"You're a little defensive."

"If you were in my place, wouldn't you be?"

She tilted her head to the side. "I suppose I would."

"Is that it?"

"For now."

He watched her for a few seconds. He should probably just get up and leave. She obviously still had her doubts about him, and he'd had enough suspicion to last a lifetime. But there was something different about her this time, as if she was leaving him an opening she hadn't before. And stupidly enough, he couldn't walk away until he knew what that was about.

"Okay, while we're being honest, answer a question for me," he said.

"If I can."

"Who was the suit in here when I arrived?"

"A county detective. He's looking into the original case I built against Dixon Hess."

"You're being investigated?"

"Yes."

"Are you worried?"

"About the investigation? No."

"About solving the case?"

"It keeps me up at night."

"And you think I can help."

"I hope so. I need it."

"Why the change? The first time, talking to you was reminiscent of the Spanish Inquisition. Now you're asking for my help?"

"I think we got off on the wrong foot."

"You accused me of murder."

"And I'm not certain if you're innocent now."

Now he really didn't know what she was up to. He took a sip from his cup to cover up the fact that he had no idea what to say. The powdered creamer congealed on the top in clumps, making for an all-around unpleasant coffee drinking experience.

"You look confused," she said.

"You got me there."

"I've decided to be straight with you in hopes that you'll be straight with me."

Now that was a change. "And how does it seem to be working so far?"

"Pretty well, I think. You?"

"I don't have a clue."

"I have a few more questions then, if that's all right."

He settled back in his chair. No doubt, he should get the hell out of here while he still could. If his lawyer was present, Lund was sure that would be his advice. But he was starting to find Chief Ryker's honesty game fascinating. He wanted to see what happened next. "Shoot."

"Why did Kelly start seeing Dixon Hess?"

"You asked me that two years ago."

"Checking to see if you've gained any insight."

"Insight? Not me. My shrink thought she was looking for someone to treat her the way she was comfortable being treated. Going back to what she knew and all that."

"Her father. The abuse."

He nodded.

"And what do you think?"

Now she sounded like his shrink. "I think that seems too simple. Like something he pulled from a damn textbook."

"When she came to see you right before she disappeared, what did she say?"

"I never told you she came to see me."

"But she did?"

"You're guessing, aren't you?"

"Yes. But only because I knew you were lying about that the first time. It was one of the things that put you at the top of my suspect list."

He couldn't help giving a little chuckle. "Is this some sort of good cop/good cop technique you're using on me? Or is it bad then, good now?"

"I'm being straightforward, like I promised."

He heaved a deep breath. Now that Kelly's body hadn't been the one in the burning barrel, he supposed what happened that night didn't matter. "Yeah, she came to see me."

"Did she tell you her plans?"

"That she was going to run away? Somehow fake her death? No."

"She didn't ask for help?"

"Not in so many words."

"What do you mean by that?"

"When I look back on it, I think that's probably why she came to me, but I didn't see it at the time." And ever since, he'd regretted letting Kelly down.

Val rubbed her right hand for a moment, as if buying time to come up with her next question. "Were you intimate that night?"

He probably should feel offended. Two years ago, he would have. Hell, an hour ago. Now, it was part of the game. You tell me yours, I tell you mine. "Sex was the way Kelly got what she wanted. My shrink had a theory about that, too."

Her gaze shifted, to the front of her desk, to her hands folded in her lap, seemingly anywhere but at him.

Finally he broke the silence. "Did I pass the test?"

She nodded.

"Then it's my turn."

"Okay."

"Do you believe I'm a killer?"

"I don't have any evidence that proves you are."

"That's not what I asked."

"Do I believe it?"

"Do you?"

She scanned his eyes, but this time her scrutiny didn't make him uncomfortable in the least.

"Well?" he prompted.

"No, I don't. I have a few things left to sort through, but I can't see it. I haven't been able to for a while now."

He had the desire to ask her to repeat what she'd just said, make sure he hadn't imagined it. Being suspected of Kelly's murder the first time had shaken him. It had been so foreign to his own perception of who he was, and he'd been powerless to change it.

Even with the qualifier, he felt as if Val Ryker had just given him something precious.

"You still want my help?"

She nodded.

"Then tell me what you want me to do."

Chapter
Nine

Val pushed herself up from the chair and forced her feet to carry her to the other side of her desk. She was in trouble. If she didn't want to realize it before, she had no choice but to face it now.

She liked David Lund far too much. What she'd told him was the truth, she believed him in spite of the fact that circumstances said she shouldn't. Enough that she wanted to tell him about Kelly's baby, even though until she knew more, it wouldn't be wise. Instead she slid the folder holding the Jane Doe photos across the blotter.

He flipped it open and looked down at the charred fragments of bone they'd recovered from the farm's burn barrel." You know, I don't have enough training to make more than basic observations."

"Your basic observations are far beyond mine. And I heard you work cheap."

"So this is a budget issue?"

"Take a look around. What do *you* think."

He gave her a grin she felt as a flutter in her chest. "You get what you pay for. I have an understanding of fire. My grasp of the human body isn't quite as firm."

She wasn't sure if he was serious or flirting, and the fact that she wanted it to be flirting bothered her even more. "If you find something that might help, I'll find the money to consult a forensic anthropologist."

He turned his focus back to the bones. No sign of guilt, of excitement, of anything other than studious concentration.

When he finished, she handed him the second file.

His lips tightened and brows lowered, but after the initial reaction to the mutilated and burned flesh, his face settled into the same unflappable focus he'd shown with the bones. Finally he closed the file and set both of them on her desk, side by side.

"Well?"

"I'm not sure what you want me to say."

"You've compared the two. Have you noticed differences?"

"Of course. You should contact a forensic anthropologist. Maybe you can use this investigation to go through the county or the state, have them foot the bill."

"Appreciate the suggestions, but I didn't ask you here for budgeting advice. Explain what you see."

"Okay. How much do you know about combustion?"

"High school science."

"Okay, think of fire as a living thing. It needs four things to exist, and if it's deprived of any of those things, it dies."

"Fuel, heat, oxygen, and...what else?"

"A chemical oxidation that causes the reaction to be self-sustaining."

She liked talking about something as defined as science. It had rules that emotion couldn't change.

Of course, police work did, too. "Explain."

"Okay. Fire takes two forms, flaming and smoldering." He held up one hand, then reached into his pocket with the other, pulled out a stainless steel lighter and flipped it open. A flick of his thumb and a small yellow flame danced at the top.

"I never pegged you for a smoker."

He gave her another grin. "I always carry one in my pocket and one on my uniform, but not for lighting up. I use it for demonstrations, at schools, that kind of thing."

"Or for the police chief." She pulled her gaze from his eyes and focused on the fire. "I'm sorry. Go on."

"Notice how the flame seems to be dancing in mid air."

"It's burning the lighter fluid."

"Fluid, right. It's a liquid which must transform into a gas before it can burn. That's why it looks like it's floating in space. It's burning the gas." He held out a hand. "I need a piece of paper."

She ripped a sheet from the legal pad in front of her and gave it to him.

He held the lighter's flame to the corner, and the paper caught fire. "Now paper is a solid, but if you look at the flame, it never touches the edge."

"So fire only burns fuel in gaseous form."

"Right. And the more readily the fuel converts to gas, the hotter the fire." He pointed through the side window of her office into the station's main room. "Like those cubicles."

She looked at the ratty old walls that had been around for much longer than she had. "Fabric burns hot?"

"It's the type of fabric, plus the filler and glue. Especially glue. Something like that or that old pressed-board paneling people have in their rec rooms? A fire trap in the making." He pinched the flame on the paper's corner between his fingers. "Don't want to set off the alarm."

She eyed the sprinkler above her desk. "Thanks."

"Flame is fuel in a gaseous state burning in the presence of oxygen. It's a gas - gas reaction," he explained.

"And smoldering is solid - gas?"

"You're a star pupil. But for a solid to burn, you need oxidation of the solid fuel in direct contact with oxygen."

"Okay, you lost me."

"Think of a cigarette. When you suck oxygen through the tobacco, the fire gets hotter, glows brighter. More oxygen equals a hotter fire. But when the cigarette sits in the ash tray, it is still burning."

"It's smoldering."

"Right. And it can only continue to burn because the structure of the burning tobacco rolled in paper is porous and rigid enough to stay that way. So oxygen is in contact with the charred surface even when the cigarette is at rest and burning at a cooler temperature."

"How does that apply to human remains?"

"A substance that doesn't create a rigid porous char won't oxidize, therefore it will not smolder and won't be self-sustaining. A good example would be thermoplastics, which melt as they burn."

Again, she wasn't following. "There weren't any thermoplastics in the barrel."

"Of course, there weren't. But the best fuel in the human body is subcutaneous fat."

"The fat layer under the skin."

"Yes. Like any oil, it burns fairly efficiently, producing a flaming fire. But first it needs heat to transform it from solid to liquid to gas."

"The fire generated by the accelerant."

"Sure. And there was plenty of oxygen in the outside air, but it isn't self-sustaining without one more thing."

"A chemical oxidation. Smoldering."

"Exactly. Namely something porous and rigid. Think of oil lamps, the fat is the oil, but it doesn't sustain the burn without a wick."

"Couldn't the flesh be the wick? Or the bones?"

"It can, but the human body is mostly water. It takes time for flesh and bone to dehydrate enough to burn. The accelerant would burn off too quickly to do more than damage the skin."

"Jane Doe's bones burned."

"Quite extensively, but you weren't just asking me about Jane Doe."

Lund stood up and flipped open the file from Nebraska. Leaning over the desk, he pointed at one of the photos. "You see this?"

His head was only inches from hers. Trying not to notice, she stared at the girl's lower calves and ankles where muscle was charred as well as the skin. In the close up shot, she could see a clear glimpse of bone. "The damage is worst at her ankles."

"And her wrists." He pointed to another shot.

Val took in the damage, then looked up at him. "So something acted as a wick on her lower legs and forearms."

"My guess? She was tied."

Val looked down at the poor woman's damaged face. How frightened she must have been when she realized his plan. Tied, helpless, witnessing that look in his eyes and feeling the slashes, the searing barrel of the curling iron, the fire's heat lick her skin.

What kind of pain had she endured?

She pushed the photo to the side and returned to Jane Doe's bones. Letting out a shuddering breath, she focused on the shards, human but not. Like studying a skeleton in science class.

A shin bone tapering to an ankle. Splinters from a forearm. Small bones from the wrist.

"There's no damage."

It was a ridiculous thing to say, and the sound of the words startled her for a second. Of course there was damage. All the flesh was gone. Not one bone had escaped splintering or charring. There was the most horrible kind of damage imaginable. And yet…

Where Jane Doe should have been tied, there were no marks. Not like the deep damage on the body in Nebraska.

"So she wasn't tied."

Hess's words spun through her mind.

If you look hard enough at the evidence in that case—not what the cops made up—you'll see it all doesn't tie together like you want it to.

"Why didn't we see this before?"

"Because you weren't looking. Listen, there are a lot of variables with fire. The conditions of the fire itself can change everything about the appearance of the remains."

Val took a photo of the Nebraska victim in one hand and Jane Doe in the other. "So what other differences do you see?"

"There is a lot of splintering of the bone."

Obviously he was talking about Jane Doe. "What does that mean?"

"It could mean a number of different things, depending on the fire conditions. But in this case, I'd guess the bones were fairly dry."

"Which means?"

"Maybe there was no need to tie her, because she was dead before she burned, maybe long before."

She scrolled through a mental list of Kelly Ann's maternal relatives. "As in dead and buried?"

"It's possible."

Val set the photos down and cradled her head in her hands. A fuzziness was beginning to form in her right eye, and the stiffness in her neck was getting worse. Her symptoms were moving from her arm to other parts of her body, as they often did, especially when fueled by stress. But as frightening as the prospect of her body betraying her was, the idea that what Hess had told her might have merit bothered her even more. "He could have been telling the truth."

"Who? Hess?"

She looked up at Lund. "He might have been framed."

"By who?"

One name popped into her mind. The person who was cleared when the investigation centered on Hess.

And she was looking right at him.

"I don't know," she said.

He narrowed his dark eyes. "Don't know or don't want to tell me?"

It was a good question, a fair question. And despite her promise to be straightforward, she wasn't willing to answer it. "If I find anything, you'll be the first to know. Deal?"

He stared at her. "You're not thinking me?"

She didn't want to. He wasn't the only one with motive. If Kelly was afraid of either of the men in her life, she would have reason to fake her own death. Unfortunately Val couldn't discuss those possibilities with Lund. Not until she'd sorted through the facts and gained some perspective. Until she did, the job would be best served if she kept all she knew to herself, played it close to the vest, as her mentor had advised.

"I told you, I don't believe you killed anyone," she said. "That hasn't changed."

Chapter
Ten

The interior of The Doghouse tavern was dark compared to the sun outside, and Val had to pause to give her eyes a chance to adjust. The rumble of male voices and a wave of smoke washed over her, a unique blend of cigarette, cigar, and the stale remnants of years gone by.

Lake Loyal had enacted a smoking ban, and word was, the entire state of Wisconsin would soon follow, but that hadn't stopped Nikki Sinclair.

If the thirty-five-year-old former stripper, stage name Nikki Sin, believed in anything it was the pleasures of lighting up and men, in that order. She smoked the way most people breathed. Val had even heard her joke that the reason she'd never had kids was too much nicotine buildup in her fallopian tubes.

Truth was, Val got a kick out of Nikki. She just tried not to show it when writing her yet another ticket for breaking the ban.

"Let me guess, shot and a beer?"

Val followed the voice to behind the bar where Nikki, currently a redhead, was wiping dust off booze bottles.

"Came to see Chief Schneider."

"Not me? I'm hurt, Val. But it's probably a good thing. My budget won't allow for any more tickets this month." She waved the bar rag in the direction of the private room off the main bar.

Eyes more accustomed to the gloom, Val followed a trail of cigar smoke through the scattered seating and circled the pool table. The double doors originally sectioning off the parlor from the rest of the house gaped open.

Val focused on the group of five men clustered around one of the tables. One puffing on a cigarette and two on cigars, they were all in their seventies, and Val knew each one. Only two of them were retired, but all found time to play a few hands of sheepshead every afternoon, almost without exception.

"Hey Val, pull up a chair," said Dick Maher, a dairy farmer who hung out at Nikki Sin's for a while before the evening milking.

"Thanks, but I have to talk to the chief." Usually it bothered her that Schneider would always be police chief in this town, but with this crowd, there was no point in insisting otherwise.

Fruehauf, the fire chief, threw a queen of clubs on the table and chuckled. "Pay up before you go, Jeff. I've got to be getting back."

By the time the men finished the hand and settled up their fifty-cents-a-point debts, Val felt like climbing out of her skin.

The chief pushed himself away from the table and stood up, brushing pretzel crumbs from his belly. "So what do you need, Val?"

She motioned him through the door and into the kitchen.

Nikki looked up from her ashtray, arching her eyebrows at their entrance.

"Can we use your back room?" Val asked.

She blew out a puff of smoke. "You owe me."

"Always."

Nikki hoisted herself up from her desk chair and pushed through the door leading to the front bar, smoke trailing in her wake.

Val cracked the back door open a sliver to let in fresh air, then turned to face the chief. "I don't think Hess killed our Jane Doe."

For a second, Schneider just stared at her, then he sputtered out a cough. "What makes you say that?"

She cut right to the comparison. Where Lund's explanation seemed more or less clear, hers sounded confusing and convoluted, even to her own ears. Still, when she finished, the chief was nodding.

"Have you asked Harlan to look into this? No offense, but you're hardly an expert, Val."

"Just called him." She skipped the part about Lund originally telling her the things she had struggled to impart. Knowing the source would only make Schneider write off the theory without examination. "Harlan's going to send the remains and the Nebraska files to a forensic anthropologist."

"Not sure it's worth all that."

"If Hess didn't kill her, we need to find who did."

He waved his hands, as if erasing her words from the air. "Of course, we do. I'm just not convinced what you've told me proves he didn't do it."

The last thing she wanted was for Hess to be innocent, and she realized that was the reason she'd decided to tell the chief this new wrinkle. If there was a flaw in the direction of her thoughts, she could rely on him to find it. "Go on."

"You say he tortured that woman in Nebraska. What's to say he didn't torture the woman up here, too? Torture her to death? Then there wouldn't be a need to tie her."

"That doesn't explain away the dryness of the bones."

He blew out an exasperated breath, his neck growing red above the collar of his shirt. "Why can't you listen?"

She knew the chief had a temper, she'd witnessed it before, but it had been ages since he'd been this irritated with her. Maybe she was jumping to conclusions and needed to slow down. "Sorry, I'm a little tightly wound lately. Go ahead."

"I'm not sure your whole dry bones theory has relevance. He could have just kept pouring on more accelerant when the fire died down. The farm is pretty remote. Your house is closest. He didn't have to worry about being caught."

She wasn't sure if that was an insult or an unfortunate choice of words, but she chose to let it slide.

"I know you're desperate, Val." His heavy brows dipped low, making him look as grim as she felt. "And I know the county has launched its investigation, but you have your killer. Thrashing around like this is only going to help his attorneys."

He was right, of course, and maybe that's what Hess truly wanted. But she needed to be sure. She decided to test her first theory. "I think there was a possibility Kelly herself was involved."

"You think she murdered and burned someone in her own family?"

"Or dug up a body to fake her own death."

He granted her a reluctant nod. "Any other theories? How about David Lund?"

The part of the conversation Val had been dreading. "I suppose it's possible he set Hess up, too."

"Damn straight, it is. Hess was running around with his wife. That's motive. He had access to the farm and no alibi—opportunity. He knows fire inside and out—means. In fact, if you're so eager to overlook Hess—which is a mistake—Lund is your guy for both murders."

Val bit the inside of her lip. She couldn't argue with any of it. So why did she want to so badly?

"Have you checked the cemeteries?" Schneider asked, moving on to the next order of business.

"I've made some calls, but the only one I've actually checked is Sunrise Ridge."

"If I remember, they're rural cemeteries and not very lavish ones. If someone dug up a grave and didn't professionally replace the dirt and sod, the ground might still show it. Listen, I'll have some time tomorrow, and I have the list Pete compiled. A little road trip sounds fun."

"That would be fantastic, Jeff. Thank you."

"Not a problem. But I want something in exchange."

"Of course. Anything."

"I want you to take care of yourself."

"Don't tell me, Oneida asked you to give me a lecture on getting more sleep?"

He chuckled. "She was always after me, too. I swear that woman is a force of nurture."

It felt good to smile. "Well, I promise to sleep when I can, how's that?"

"A good idea, but sleep is not exactly what I had in mind."

"What?"

"Keep this whole Hess-is-innocent theory quiet. And ask Harlan to hold off on contacting the forensic anthropologist, at least for now."

"I can't just cover this up, Jeff."

His jaw hardened and hands formed fists by his side. "I'm not saying you should. Just give us time to dig up more evidence. Don't go off half-cocked. You're under investigation, Val. You have a lot to lose. Just make sure when you're looking out for truth and justice, you look out for yourself too. Because no one can to do it for you. That includes me."

Val hadn't even reached her office when Oneida's voice boomed through the station. "Monica Forbes is waiting, line one."

Her mind was still buzzing over her talk with Jeff Schneider, and although he'd laid out like trump cards all the reasons why she should suspect Lund, she didn't feel clearer headed than she had before she'd set foot in the Doghouse.

"She said it's urgent," Oneida called.

Val waved her acknowledgement, slipped into her office, and shut the door. Not bothering to take off her coat, she raced directly to her desk, and picked up the phone. "Monica."

"He called me."

Val didn't ask who. "Did he threaten you?"

"He's too careful, but he didn't have to. He phoned our hotel room, Val. At the casino. How could he know I was here?"

If Hess's aim was to frighten, he was succeeding. Val had to say something to calm the district attorney down. She needed Monica to think logically. "It's not a secret you like the casino. You weren't home, so he went to the next option on his list."

"The fact that he has a list is what disturbs me. I don't like him knowing so much about me."

Val had to agree. "Exactly what did he say?"

"He asked me if I believed in justice. That was it, just that one question."

"He asked me the same thing. And Tamara Wade."

"His own lawyer?"

"Maybe he didn't think she did a good job."

"She did a fine job. She just lost. But then, she was up against me, so who can blame her?"

Val let out a breath she wasn't aware she'd been holding. "Calming down, Monica?"

"I guess. Yeah." Monica laughed, the sound deep and throaty. "I was pretty freaked out, wasn't I?"

"Can't say I blame you. I think freaked out is just where Hess wants us."

"Has he threatened anyone else?"

"I'm only aware of the three of us, but the day is still young." As she said the words, the line two indicator light started blinking. "I'll keep you posted, Monica."

"Call my cell. Derrick took more of his vacation, so we're staying a couple more days, trying out a few more positions. Gambling has given him stamina like you wouldn't believe."

"Right. Ah, okay, have fun." She cut off the call.

Line two was Oneida. "A call just came in. I figured you'd want to know."

"Who?"

"A student at the high school. Dixon Hess is there …"

Val was on her feet before she heard the rest.

"… and she thinks he has a gun."

Chapter
Eleven

"Shots fired?" Val called to Oneida, running past dispatch on her way out.

"No. Becca's en route."

"Call county. We'll need help. And maybe Baraboo can spare someone. EMS, too."

"On it."

She felt cooler, calmer than she had any right to, but she knew that was thanks to years of training. Adrenaline made the world around her laser sharp and brittle. Grace's beautiful face flashed through her mind, but she resisted giving into the accompanying feelings.

Sharp. Focus.

She grabbed a vest on her way out and ran for her car. She didn't have lights and sirens, but the school was only blocks away. Pushing the speed limit as much as she dared, she made it in minutes.

The one story high school was quiet, no movement, no sound, doors all closed. Becca was already there. Standing at the rear of her black-and-white, trunk open, her body visibly shaking.

Val ditched her coat in the car and was out of the vehicle nearly the moment it stopped. Making straight for Becca, she shrugged on the Kevlar. "Have you made contact with anyone?"

"Oneida has a teacher on the phone now. But she doesn't seem to know anything."

"School locked down?"

"Yes."

"The teacher, did she see a gun?"

"She saw something, not really sure it was a gun. Maybe we should wait."

"That's not how it works, Becca."

Since the Columbine High School tragedy, law enforcement had changed tactics in cases like this. No more holding the perimeter. No more waiting for a hostage negotiator or tactical team. Confronting an active shooter was all about going in as quickly as possible.

Limiting the damage. Eliminating the threat.

Becca should know all of this, she'd gone through the training, but the way her hands shook as she pulled the school floor plan out of her squad bag explained the lapse.

Not a good sign. "Damn, where's county?"

Becca tapped the mic clipped to the shoulder of her uniform and relayed the question to Oneida.

"On their way," came the answer.

"How many?"

"A county deputy, one officer from Baraboo and one from Lake Delton, provided he can get there in time. EMS should be there any minute."

As if on cue, the screech of sirens rode the cold wind.

Good. That would be four officers without Becca. As jittery as she was, Val wasn't sure she trusted the rookie to handle the situation.

But they'd better hurry.

So far the news didn't seem to be out. Once another kid snuck a call on a cell phone, the place would doubtlessly be flooded with parents rushing in to save their children.

Like Val was doing now.

She forced herself to breathe, to think. Spreading out the map, she studied the school's simple floor plan, even though she already had it committed to memory. "What classroom?"

"He was last seen entering the four hundred wing," Oneida said. "That's all I got."

Sirens grew louder, then shut off abruptly. Two cars pulled into the parking lot, one from the county sheriff's department, one from the Baraboo PD. They positioned the vehicles to cut off the entrances, lights flashing, and joined Val at Becca's car.

Going over the map with them took only a few seconds. As she talked, she tightened the Velcro straps on her vest. Dead hand giving her problems, the county deputy finally had to help.

"Thanks. Injured it."

"Better take a rifle."

She took the rifle from Becca's squad and told the others about the officer en route from Lake Delton.

"There are four of us here now. We can't wait." Val eyed Becca. "You okay?"

"Yes."

"You looked a little shaken."

"I'm fine." She nodded to underscore. "I was kind of upset, but I'm better, getting it under control."

Val studied her for a moment. Her breathing seemed only slightly elevated, the shaking not as pronounced. "Okay, I'll take you at your word. Let's go."

The rifle felt awkward in her hand, but it was a big improvement from her 9mm. With Becca on the radio, at least she didn't have to handle that.

Val led, approaching the school from the entrance at the end of the four hundred wing's hallway. She could see into the glass doors. No one in the hall. "Going in."

Becca did her parrot act for Oneida's benefit.

The door wasn't locked. The deputy yanked it open, and they streamed in, single file. Val and Becca moved close to the right wall. The deputy and Baraboo cop took the left.

The hallway stretched long in front of them, sun from the other end glowing off the waxed and polished floor. The hall was neat, no scattered papers or backpacks, as if it was a normal school day, everyone in class, nothing out of place.

There had still been no report of gunfire, and Val had to wonder why. If Hess had the recklessness to burst into a school with a gun, why hadn't he used it? What was he planning?

Each classroom had a solid door with a side panel of glass, similar to her office back at the station. They moved to the first door, the other two taking the classroom opposite. A peek inside showed the kids at their desks. The teacher was the only one standing, the only adult in the room. An older woman with a pinched-looking face met Val's eyes. She held a cell phone in her hand and gestured to it. The one on the phone with Oneida.

"This room's clear." Val glanced across the hall.

"This one's empty," called the deputy.

They moved on to the next class. On Val and Becca's side, this room was also filled with kids. The teacher, a man, rushed to the door as if to throw it open. She held up her hand. "Keep it locked."

He nodded and stood staring at her, hands hanging limp at his sides.

"Clear over here," the deputy said.

Third door down.

She peered in. The first thing she noticed was Grace's face. The second was Hess's.

They were several feet apart, Grace sitting at a desk, Hess standing at the front of the class. But as far as Val was concerned, Dixon Hess being in the same building as her niece was too close for her comfort.

"Got him." She nodded to Becca for the pliers.

The rookie fumbled at her belt. The tool hit the floor with a clang.

The other two were beside them, the Baraboo cop using his pliers on the doorknob. A hard twist, and they were in.

Val led with the rifle. "Get down. Now. All of you, down."

Kids screamed. Other officers barked orders. The teacher threw herself in front of students near her, pushing them to the floor.

Hess smiled and held his hands up.

His *empty* hands.

She leveled the rifle straight on the bastard's upper lip. She wasn't positive she could rely on her fingers to pull the trigger, but if he so much as twitched, she'd damn well find a way. "On the floor."

He flattened himself on his stomach.

"Hands on your head. Ankles crossed."

He assumed the position like an old pro.

"Somebody cuff him."

The deputy stepped forward and secured Hess's hands behind his back. Once that was done, he ran his hands over the bound man's sides and down his legs. "He's clean."

"What did you do with the gun?"

"You think I'm armed?" Hess's voice was far more calm than it should be. He tilted his eyes up and met Val's. "Why would I bring a gun into the school? You think I'm suicidal?"

"Face down."

"I think someone's feeding you bad information, Chief Val."

She hadn't felt anything but clear and focused on her way into the school, riding a wave of adrenaline. Now her pulse was thrumming so hard she couldn't think, and her whole body was vibrating.

She located Grace in the group of kids being ushered from the room by the Baraboo cop. She was okay. Unhurt. Her niece was all that really mattered.

And now Hess knew it, too.

Chapter
Twelve

Val eyed her officers gathered in the police station's conference room. "How in the hell did he get invited to speak at the school? And why didn't anyone in the office seem to know about it?"

Now that Hess was safely contained in the single holding cell, Val couldn't contain her disbelief. How could they have possibly raided the high school on a misunderstanding? How many failures had to stack up for that to happen? How many people didn't do their jobs?

"It wasn't an accident," Pete Olson said. Hearing what was going on, he'd rushed to the high school on his day off.

Val had been glad for the help. "You know that for a fact, Pete?"

"Not for a fact. But the girl who called it in? There's something fishy there, something she's not telling. I can't say if she's lying about the gun or Hess made her think he had one. Either way, after all this town has gone through, he had to know he'd stir up a panic setting foot in that school and bypassing the office. And then there was the specific classroom he chose."

Val felt cold. She turned her head, trying to stretch the spasm from her neck muscles and not think too hard about how close Hess had gotten to Grace. Leaving her niece at school to finish out the rest of the day had been one of the hardest things she'd ever done, even knowing Hess would be locked up in their holding cell until after the final bell rang.

Still she'd arranged for the second shift officer to pick up her niece from school and bring her to the station. Grace wouldn't be happy, but she'd get over it. Val wasn't taking chances. She'd also ramped up her efforts to get Grace out of town.

"The classroom teacher said she invited him," Becca said, addressing Olson.

"I took her statement," Olson said. "Seems he happened to run into her at the supper club and gave her the idea. The bastard was hoping it would work out this way."

"Why?" Becca asked.

"To make sure Val knew he could reach Grace."

"But he couldn't control the situation. He might have been shot." Becca leaned toward Olson, her eyebrows pinched and lips pursed, as if really trying to understand, and Val couldn't help thinking she looked like Grace studying physics.

"Too bad he wasn't," Olson said.

Becca shook her head. "I interviewed the teacher Oneida had on the phone. She didn't see a gun, but she was definitely afraid. She said some things about his release, things she heard from her brother."

"Her brother?"

"Derrick Shaw."

Val shifted the name around in her mind until it fell into place. "Monica Forbes's fiancé?"

Becca nodded.

Damn small towns. Everyone connected. Everyone knowing everyone else's business. Derrick Shaw runs his mouth off, and panic grows. "What about the teacher who invited Hess to class? Did she clear it with anyone?"

"The office knew she invited a guest, but not who."

It sounded like a setup, all right. And she needed to talk to the one monster who could explain it all. *If* he wanted to.

"Finish up the paperwork. And don't talk to the media, not yet. I'll be giving an official statement in time for the six o'clock news." Val left the conference room and slipped into dispatch.

Oneida had ducked into the adjoining office for the moment, donning her clerical hat, the only sign of her a plate of her famous red and green iced sugar cookies under a monitor showing the location of the two squads currently out on the road, one having already picked up Grace from school.

Val grabbed a reindeer and glanced at another monitor mounted high on the wall. The screen was split into four images, the entry door outside, the squad parking area and entrance for officers, the area outside the holding cell, and the holding cell itself. Hess sat on the concrete bench, leaning back against the wall, as if dozing.

She was just about to turn away when he opened his eyes and looked directly at the camera. The urge to step back, out of his line of vision, was overwhelming.

Stupid. He couldn't see her, the camera image only went one way, and yet she could feel his eyes on her as distinct as a physical touch.

"I suppose we have to release him then?"

She started at Becca's voice. "I'm afraid so," Val said.

"I'll take care of it."

"No need." The thought of Hess anywhere near the rookie while not in cuffs made Val sweat almost as much as seeing him in the same room as Grace. "Go ahead and clock out. And have a cookie." She handed the reindeer to Becca.

Becca turned toward the staircase leading to the basement briefing room and lockers. Before she took the first step, she turned back. "I overheard some of what you and Mr. Lund were talking about this morning." She held up her hands as if to ward off any anger that might be coming her way. "I didn't mean to. I didn't eavesdrop or anything, but—"

"What did you overhear?"

"That things, um, might not be what you thought. That Hess might not—"

Val held up a palm, cutting her off. "You can't tell anyone about that."

"I won't."

"I don't yet know if there's any truth to it."

"Okay. I won't say anything, but remember, whatever you need, even if I'm not on the clock."

Val couldn't help but give the rookie a smile. "Actually, I do have something."

The rookie beamed. "What?"

"You can canvass hospitals for me. We're trying to find out if Kelly Lund checked in during the past year, and we've only made a small dent in the list so far."

"I'll get started right away."

"First tell Oneida to turn on the camera for the interrogation room."

Becca took a bite of cookie then scampered out the door with a bounce in her stride that Val wished she could harness to boost her flagging energy.

She met Oneida on her way to the holding cell. The idea of watching Dixon Hess walk out of custody for the second time in as many days weighed on her, but there was no alternative. She had no reason to hold him. And the last thing they needed was for him to still be in custody when the press arrived.

She checked her weapon into the gun safe next to the door. Like sheriff's deputies operating the local jail and corrections officers in state prison, her officers were never around unsecured prisoners while armed. It felt risky, yet she knew it would be much riskier if Hess was to get his hands on her gun.

Not that he could get out even if he was armed. Not unless Oneida buzzed open the doors from the dispatch center.

She stepped through the door and onto the painted concrete floor, the lock securing behind her. The room smelled of disinfectant, a strange mix of lemon, rubbing alcohol and hospital. In a town the size of Lake Loyal, they only had one holding cell, and it was generally used by the handful of drunks who insisted on driving or starting fights, and locking up drunks always made for a bevy of unpleasant smells.

Hearing the lock clank closed behind her, she glanced up at the camera positioned to catch everything that happened outside the holding cell. Next to it, another monitor showed Hess inside the cell.

No longer staring at the camera, he looked small, ordinary. If she'd been passing him on the street, she might not have even noticed him. That might be what she found most disconcerting of all.

She crossed to the single cell and opened the door.

He remained sitting, reaching his arms over his head in an exaggerated stretch. "Ahh. Freedom is never dear at any price. It is the breath of life. What would a man not pay for living? Do you know who said that?"

He focused on her, his gaze so intense, it was all she could do to keep from looking away.

"I'd like to have a word with you. Is your lawyer on her way?"

"Gandhi," he continued. "I had a lot of time to read in prison. Got to fully understand all that was taken from me. He and I are a lot alike."

"You're comparing yourself to Gandhi?"

He shrugged and rose to his feet. "You want to talk? Let's talk."

Val stood to the side, allowing him to step into the secured area outside the cell. She gestured to a small room with a short table jutting from one wall and benches secured on either side. Made of coated steel, it came complete with thick rings in the frame for attaching cuffs and leg shackles.

He sat down, hands and legs free.

"Do you want to wave your right to an attorney?"

One side of his mouth crooked upward. "I think I already have."

That was easier than she expected. "Why did you go to the high school today?"

"I was asked to speak. And do you know what I was asked to speak about?"

She didn't answer.

"Justice."

"Did you bring a weapon into the school?"

"A weapon? Why would I do that?"

He was having far too much fun with the question for her to believe his innocent act. "When you walked in, you had something in your hand. What was it?"

"Just some construction paper."

"Let me guess, construction paper made to look like a gun?"

"Of course not. It was a harmless piece of paper. Whoever told you it was a gun has quite an imagination."

He'd either set the girl up, or convinced her to help him with his charade. "I thought you didn't play games."

"I don't. Everything I do is very real."

"No, me nearly putting a bullet in your head today, that was real."

He chuckled.

She knew Hess had balls. She didn't realize they were the size of cantaloupe. "Don't push me. Shooting you would be a treat. I see what you are, what you did to that girl in Nebraska."

"You looked at the files? Did you notice any differences?"

"She was tied."

"Very good."

"So you could torture her, burn her."

"I didn't do anything. A jury found me not guilty, remember?"

Okay, she'd keep it hypothetical. "Why does someone do something like that? What possesses them to do something so evil?"

His lips tightened, and he shook his head. "People deserve to get what they dish out. Eye for an eye. The thief who steals loses his hand, that sort of thing."

"Justice."

He shot her a wide grin, showing those perfect teeth. "Exactly."

"What did that girl do to you?"

"Nothing. Except suck my dick. She was pretty good at that."

Val kept her expression neutral. "She was the thing someone loved the most, wasn't she? Who was that someone?"

"And you said you read the police reports?"

She thought about the reports, the transcripts of the trial. "Her father."

Hess smiled. "What is the point of revenge if the person you want to hurt isn't around to enjoy the pain? At least for a little while."

"You tortured a girl to death to get back at her father?"

He tapped his chest with his fingertips. "Not guilty, remember?"

"What did he do to you?"

He crossed his arms over his chest.

"At trial, the prosecutor argued that the girl refused to date you."

"If by date you mean open her legs, she dated anything that moved."

"I could ask the father. His number is in the police report."

"He wasn't a good man, Chief Val. Whatever happened to him, he deserved it."

"Okay, I'll ask him to explain."

"Do that. And while you're at it, ask what he did to Rascal."

"Rascal?"

"A kid's best friend is his dog."

His dog. The neighbor had done something to his dog, so Hess had tortured and killed the man's daughter. Dixon Hess's version of justice.

"It was nice meeting the kids at school today. All those fresh faces, bright futures. Especially this blond beauty. I think her name was Grace."

Val leaned close. "You touch her, you're dead."

The intercom gave a light buzz. "Chief?" Oneida said over the speaker.

"Go ahead. Answer." Hess smiled. "I think we're done here anyway."

Chapter
Thirteen

Val completed the details of Hess's release as quickly as she could, and when she got back to dispatch, she was still shaking.

Oneida, too, looked more pale than usual. "Mr. Haselow has called an emergency meeting."

It had to be about what had happened at the high school. Typical for the village president to hold an emergency meeting after the emergency was over. "In the conference room?"

"He and The Chief are waiting for you in your office."

"Thanks, Oneida. Why don't you go home now? Your shift was done hours ago."

The big woman shook her head hard enough to send her earrings jangling. "No chance. Not until everything's back to normal around here."

Val had the sense that things wouldn't return to normal until Hess either killed again and was caught or moved on. Unwilling to lay that kind of pessimism on poor Oneida, she resigned herself to a lame nod. "Then you probably won't be getting home for quite a while."

"I have tomorrow off. I can sleep then."

"Working all the time, not getting proper rest, you're as bad as I am."

Oneida gave her a wink. "But I smell sweeter."

She probably had a point.

And when Val entered her office and was almost knocked over by a wave of cologne that reeked as if it had passed some kind of expiration date and soured like milk, her first thought was to make sure the odor wasn't coming from her.

The village president, a skinny little balding man named Haselow who never seemed to like Val very much, gave her a screamingly phony smile. "So glad you're finally here. I guess we can start the meeting then."

Lounging in one of the chairs in front of her desk, Jeff Schneider pressed his lips together. Not a smile exactly, but a show of support, subtle as it may be.

She circled to the power side of the desk and sat. "Sorry for keeping you waiting. It's been busy."

"So we've heard." Haselow perched on the edge of his chair. The man was nervous, always moving, a jiggling leg, shifting eyes, hand fiddling with his suit jacket.

Just watching him exhausted her. How he'd convinced people to vote for him, she'd never know.

"All the news outlets are covering it," he rattled on. "It's very unfortunate. We are very concerned."

Val laid out the facts of the afternoon, trying to keep her voice even and reassuring; Hess's gun that turned out to be paper, the way he'd wheedled a speaking invitation in her niece's class, the fact that they'd secured the building without anyone getting hurt.

Schneider nodded understandingly.

Haselow seemed to grow more nervous. "Oh, that's bad. Very bad. It seems we should have made this move as soon as that girl was found in the lake."

"This move?"

Schneider folded his hands in his lap.

Haselow fluttered out of his chair and crossed the room in short strides.

"You're planning to fire me?"

"Heavens, no."

"Ask me to resign?"

The village president waved his hands. "Nothing like that."

"Then what?"

"I really hate to do this, but after great deliberation, I think it's the only sensible solution. Lake Loyal has to know that during this difficult time, it can still rely on its police department."

She wished he would just spit it out. "I'm fired?"

"Oh, no, no, no," Haselow shook his head as if that conclusion was the silliest thing he'd heard all day. "You're suspended. With pay. Just until the county can complete its investigation."

And then she would be fired.

"And I'm putting myself on this suspension?"

Now the bobble head switched to an incessant nod. "After the stressful situation at the school, you thought it best if someone else was in charge for now."

"Then I should probably be impressed with myself. Who knew I was so level headed, selfless, and responsible?"

Schneider cracked a hint of a smile.

Haselow switched back to shaking head mode and glanced longingly at the door.

She forced herself to breathe, in and out, in and out. How had she failed to see this coming? Now she had no clue how to deal with it. She stepped to the front of her desk and leaned a hip on the edge. She couldn't just walk away. Suspended or not, she felt responsible for the town's safety.

Now more than ever.

Maybe she could work with the interim chief. Maybe she could convince him to let her help, even if it was on her own time. "Who's taking over the department?"

Haselow glanced around the room, shoulders hitched up around his ears. He looked like a frightened mouse, too frightened, apparently, to come out with it.

She looked up at Chief Schneider. "Who?"

He gave her an apologetic smile. "It will all be okay, Val. Don't worry about it."

"You?"

"It'll work out. For everyone."

Val wasn't sure if she was supposed to feel betrayed or relieved, but—as seemed to be happening a lot lately— all she could muster was numb.

"If you have any concerns, anything I should be aware of, don't hesitate to let me know," said Schneider.

Concerns? Was he kidding? She'd just spilled her list of concerns to him this morning. Concerns he'd obviously turned around and used to convince Haselow and the board that she should be suspended.

"I'll leave you two to work out the transition." Haselow shrugged on his coat, fumbling with the sleeves. Once he finally managed to get dressed, he gave Val a strangely awkward bow.

Schneider stood and shook the man's hand. Val expected him to wipe his palm on his pants afterward, but instead, the father she always wanted circled the desk and lowered himself into her chair. He leaned back, looking at home, in control, back where he belonged.

Transition complete.

Val hardly noticed Haselow close the door behind him. "What's going on, Jeff?"

"Just trying to help."

"You think I handled things the wrong way? You think I should have just ignored a report of Dixon Hess entering the high school with a gun? Would you have ignored it?"

"I think the stresses of the past week have caught up with you, that's all. It could happen to anyone. I'm just trying to help."

She had to calm down, choose her words carefully. But at the moment, anything short of slamming her fist on the blotter and yelling seemed inadequate. "I don't need your kind of help, Jeff."

"Don't need it? Really? One minute you're telling me you don't think Dixon Hess is guilty, the next you're almost shooting him in front of a classroom of school children."

She opened her mouth, ready to fire back something sharp and hurtful, but the words wouldn't come. The fact was, she could understand how her words and actions wouldn't add up. "I can explain—"

"Don't have to. You've been stressed. No one is blaming you. But you're under investigation, and now with Hess stirring up trouble and the media lapping it up …" He heaved a sigh so heavy his whole body convulsed. "It's a good time to take a break. If you weren't so close to this, you'd see. Hell, you probably *would* suggest the suspension yourself."

"I do have to explain. Remember what I told you about Hess?"

He looked at her with dull eyes.

"Whether you agree doesn't matter. He's going to start killing the people he blames for putting him in prison."

"He made threats? Why haven't you arrested him?"

"He knows which words to choose to get his point across."

Schneider nodded. "He is slippery. But I'll take care of him. I know how to do the job."

She didn't think he meant to imply she didn't, but he also didn't know what he was up against, not like she did. "I'm serious. People are going to die."

"If you're trying to tell me Hess is a dangerous man, Val, believe me, I know. That's what I was trying to get across to you this morning, what Pete has been saying all along. You can't make a deal with a man like that. He played you at the school today. He's playing you on this Jane Doe case."

She wished she could argue with any of that, but until she had hard evidence, nothing she could say would convince Schneider that Hess hadn't killed Jane Doe.

She wasn't entirely convinced herself.

"The investigation will be over soon, and with me taking over the job, you won't miss a beat."

"I suppose you're right."

"I am. Now gather what you need from your office, go home, catch up on your rest, and spend some time with that niece of yours."

His suggestions sounded wonderful, if a killer's threat wasn't hanging over her town.

"Everything will be fine. Just fine," he said.

She located her coat and bag and took a last glance around her office. Staring at her from the wall above Schneider's head, hung her college diploma, certificates from Staff and Command school and the FBI's National Academy and—in the ultimate twist of office décor irony—the framed newspaper clipping announcing Hess's conviction.

"I'll bet you don't know why you're here."

Tamara Wade wasn't sure if the male voice was part of her dream or calling her out of it, but she didn't want to wake.

"I mean you didn't do anything wrong, did you? You went through the motions, stood up there in your tailored suit and your power pumps and played your part."

Not a dream. Real. And when she realized that, something inside of her cringed.

Where was she?

The place smelled musty, dank like a basement and cold. She was lying on her side, naked, hard concrete underneath, so cold her muscles twitched and jerked in shivers. She tried to open her eyes, but her lids were heavy, her head looping and spinning even though her body remained still.

"You didn't lie. Not one word. You told the truth, but not the part that would help me."

She tried to bring her hand to her face, to find out what was wrong with her eyes, to support her head, but they wouldn't reach.

Tied. Her wrists were tied.

To each other. To the floor.

A blindfold wrapped her eyes.

Where in the hell was she?

It all came back then, the parking garage, his smile when she saw him, the smile of a predator. She'd been so proud of her role in getting him out of prison, in saving a man from a punishment the state failed to prove he deserved.

Now she was the one being punished. "Am I still in the garage?"

"No."

"Where am I?"

"A place where we can have some privacy."

Privacy. To kill her. To rape her. To do whatever he pleased. "What do you want, Dixon?"

"You really weren't listening, were you?"

What had she missed? "I'm sorry. My head."

"Just talking, talking, talking. You never gave a shit about what I had to say. You still aren't listening."

"I'm sorry. I am now. I promise." Why couldn't she see? She needed to get a look at his face, read his expressions, tell him what he wanted to hear. "Please."

"Talking again. Talking instead of listening."

"I'm sorry." Her throat was going to be raw from apologizing, but she didn't know what else to do, how else to reach him. "Take the blindfold off, please. I need to see you. I can listen better if I can see you."

"Listening is done with the ears, Tamara."

"Please."

She heard the shuffle of shoes on concrete and could feel him near her. He tugged at the fabric binding her eyes, yanking her hair along with it.

A bare bulb hung from the ceiling, the energy saving kind with the pigtail curls. She blinked back the glare.

"Has your listening improved?"

She was in a basement, a pile of boxes near her head, an old bed spring leaning against the wall. Her hands were tied in front of her, fingers purple from lack of circulation. The rope securing them was fastened to a steel ring embedded in the concrete, like something from a dungeon.

Shadows surrounded her, but she still couldn't see Dixon Hess. "Where are you?"

"Behind you. Just getting a little something to help you listen."

A shudder worked over her skin, fear adding to cold until she could no longer control her muscles.

"You know what your problem is, Tamara? Why you are a shit listener?"

Her teeth chattered together, the tremor taking her. She craned her neck, trying to spot him.

"Do you?"

"What do you want me to say?"

"You always have to be talking, always talking. You can't listen if you're constantly flapping your gums."

"I'm sorry. I'm sorry."

"You still don't get it?" His voice wasn't angry but cold.

Somehow that frightened her more than anything. "Don't get what? Just tell me what to do."

"Listen."

"I'm listening. Really, I am."

"No, you're not, Tamera. You're talking. You love talking more than anything in the world. And I'm about to take that away from you."

A scream worked up the base of her throat.

And when he stepped into the light, and she saw the long sewing needle in his fingers, thread trailing from the eye, her shriek broke free.

Chapter
Fourteen

"I called a friend of mine," Val explained to her niece. "She invited us to stay with her a few days."

Grace greeted the news with a frown.

She'd been frowning since Val got home, had frowned all through dinner, and Val had to admit, she couldn't blame her. It had been a hell of an upsetting day, not just for her, but for Grace, too. And even though she felt as if she'd been run through a wringer and come out still soaking wet, she needed to hold it together. One of them had to, and it wasn't fair to expect it of a sixteen year old.

The tea pot screamed from the stove. Val tore open two packets of instant hot chocolate, dumped them into cups, and poured in the steaming water. She hadn't finished outlining the plans she made, and had yet to break the news about her suspension. She'd hoped chocolate would make everything go down a little more easily.

She carried the fragrant mugs into the adjoining living room and set them on the coffee table. "My friend is really great. You'll like her. And there's a lot of fun stuff to do in Chicago."

"Chicago?" The sixteen year old flopped herself on the couch the way only a hormonal girl facing a life upheaval could. "What about the horses?"

Val took a sip of the cocoa, burning her tongue. Giving up, she set the cup down and eyed her niece. "Oneida found a man who has horses of his own. He's agreed to feed and muck stalls while we're gone."

"What if he doesn't know what he's doing? What if Max colics again? What if he forgets to check Banshee's blanket and she gets too hot? Or too cold?"

"I think he can manage."

"How about water? If the power goes out, the heater in the water tank won't work."

"If that happens, he'll carry buckets from the house."

"The water pump in the house won't work either."

"So we'll tell him to get some jugs of water from Wal-Mart."

"Do you know how much water horses drink?"

"Did you miss the part about him having his own horses?" Val shot back.

Grace shook her head, blond hair flying. "A lot of people have horses, and they're really stupid about taking care of them."

Val forced a deep breath into her lungs. She'd hardly slept in days, and even though some feeling seemed to be returning to her hand—she hoped—the problem with her neck and head was getting worse. On the drive home from the station, she'd been hit with a fatigue so deep, she'd been barely able to make it.

Jeff Schneider had been right. She needed to get out of here, to get Grace out of here. Even if it was only a few days, she needed to make sure they were both safe so she could rest.

She could do that in Chicago.

"Listen Grace, no one cares for those horses like you do. But that doesn't mean this guy can't handle feeding and cleaning for a few days." She prayed it wouldn't be longer than that, although if her suspension turned into losing her job completely, they wouldn't have to worry about taking care of the horses. They'd have to sell them.

No point in mentioning that to Grace just now.

She stared at the empty fireplace for what seemed like forever, then wiping her eyes with the back of one hand, she pulled herself into a sitting position on the couch and folded her arms. "I want to talk to him."

Definite progress. "He'll be here for feeding time to-morrow morning. You can show him around, give him instructions."

Arms still crossed over her chest, Grace lightened up on the pout. At least a little.

"Come on. It'll be fun."

"I'm not a kid. I know this isn't just for fun. It's because of what happened in school today, isn't it?"

Val couldn't deny it.

"Heidi saw he had a gun. She did. She wouldn't lie about that."

"He was messing with her, Grace. He was messing with the teachers. He was messing with all of us."

"And now you're in trouble?"

"I was suspended, with pay. Which just means I have to take a little vacation."

"They're making you. That's not a vacation."

"It'll be fine. Jeff will take care of everything. And we'll get out of here, away from Hess and this whole mess."

"What if he follows us?"

"He won't."

"You don't know that."

She didn't. But there was a reason she chose Chicago, and it wasn't all about free lodging. "My friend? The one we're staying with? She's put away people nastier than Dixon Hess. We'll be safe there. The only thing you have to worry about is whether you want to go shopping or visit museums first."

Grace still didn't look convinced. Pointedly ignoring the steaming cup of cocoa, she grabbed the remote off the coffee table and started flipping channels.

"Still refusing to climb aboard the fun train?"

Not a smile, not even a hint.

To tell the truth, Val couldn't blame her. At the moment, it was tough to find anything to smile about. "It's going to work out, Grace. Really."

The same words Jeff Schneider had said to her.

She hadn't believed them either.

Lund was running before his boots hit the ground.

The car had skidded off the road and over a small embankment. There it had rolled, crushing through snow and into rock.

The rock didn't give. The steel did.

Having settled back on its tires, the Volvo had come to a stop against the tree trunk now embedded a foot into the hood on the driver's side. Pebbles of glass blanketed the snow, sparkling in the headlights of Unit One. The side windows were completely pulverized. The windshield remained intact, so many cracks marring the expanse, it appeared opaque.

Lund had seen a number of wrecks, and while this wasn't the worst, the driver would have to be lucky to survive. He meant to improve that luck.

Drawing close, he could make out the airbag, now deflated, and the shadow of a human form. The scent of gasoline tinged the cold air, along with the sweet hint of antifreeze. There was something else, too. The odor of burned hair.

He slid on ice, nearly fell, then righted himself before he reached the vehicle.

A woman was inside. Skull thrown back against the headrest. Her face was half covered by copper-blond hair, but he could still see the glisten of blood. There was also blood on her bare shoulder, a lot of it, and he could hear a disturbing gurgle with each breath she took.

He tried the door, but it wouldn't budge. "We're here to help. We're going to get you out. Understand?"

Another gurgle.

"I want you to stay calm." He had no idea if his words would help her, or if she was even able to process them, but he kept talking anyway.

A siren screamed from the direction of the highway, the EMTs arriving, their flashing reds adding to the police red and blue pulsing off trees and snow.

It took only seconds for him to size up the damage. The hit from the front had forced the fender and front wheel back into the passenger compartment, making the door useless. Normally they would remove the roof, peel it back and lay it out on the hood. It would provide clear access to the victim, but the process was time consuming, and he didn't need to be an EMT to know time wasn't something this woman had.

The hydraulic pump growled to life.

Dempsey, Johnson and a young guy named Blaski tromped down the bank and scrambled over rock, their arms weighed down with tools. Johnson set up lights illuminating the scene as best they could.

Dempsey's breath fogged the air. "How's it look?"

"We're going to have to take off the door," Lund said.

Dempsey nodded and brandished his weapon of choice, a hydraulic cutting tool with curved blades that resembled the bill of a parrot, if your average parrot could bite through the toughest steel. The tool was heavy, but other than that, it took little strength to operate, thanks to hydraulics. The challenge to using it was knowing where to place the blade. The wrong spot and a rescuer could easily hit belt pretensioners, gas shocks or set off one of the side airbags.

A mechanic by trade, Dempsey knew his cars. He opened the steel jaws and punched one blade through the windshield, then cut through the point connecting the car's roof to its body. Another cut to the rear of the driver's window frame, and the pressure from the roof was no longer a factor.

Lund took the spreader from Blaski. Larger and heavier, this tool did exactly as the name suggested, splaying steel as easily as if it was Playdoh. He fitted the device between the front fender and the driver's door and got to work. The arms moved outward, slow but steady. Soon he could see the hinges. The first one popped under the pressure. The second, Dempsey had to cut. They lifted off the door.

She was even worse than he'd expected.

The dashboard had folded inward. Her legs seemed to bend backwards, not just at the knee, but like a comma from mid-thigh to ankle. Completely naked, her body was marred by more burns and cuts than Lund could count. In places, she was raw and oozy red, shiny in the lights, the first few layers of skin gone. Nylon cord fastened her wrists, and when he tilted her head back to check for a pulse, he saw her lips.

At first they appeared to be bloody and clustered with wiry flies. Then he realized her mouth was sewn shut.

"Holy shit," Dempsey said.

Lund's reaction exactly.

He pulled his focus from the woman and directed it to the car's structure, trying not to think too much about damage done to flesh and bone. Trying to concentrate on how best to roll the dashboard forward to take pressure off her legs. But even though he'd become a master at compartmentalizing over the years, he could still feel a tremor run along every nerve, shaking him to the core.

Holy shit was right.

He moved the spreader's arms together until he could fit them between the car's floor and the dash. Despite the cold air, sweat trickled down his back under the insulated turnout gear. Holding the heavy device in place, he let the hydraulics do their thing. The steel frame shifted, tilting the dash back, the wheel up to face the crushed roof.

The progress was slow, too slow.

His face shield fogged with his breath, and he flipped it up. Out of the corner of his eye, he could see movement coming down the hill, the techs and their equipment, silhouettes against the flashing, glaring lights.

Her pulse had been hard to find, the beat light and erratic.

He prayed she was still alive by the time he pried her free.

Chapter
Fifteen

Val might not be acting police chief, but she still had her radio.

When she heard the call go out about a car off the road in the bluffs on the east side of town, she hadn't thought much about it. But when a steady and experienced Lake Loyal officer named Christopher Edgar had called in a breathless request for the shift sergeant and Chief Schneider to meet him at the scene, Val woke Grace, and the two of them piled into the Focus.

Since the Crown Vic she usually drove belonged to the police department, she'd had to leave that behind along with her service pistol. She didn't mind driving the Focus, but the pistol she felt naked without. She'd have to go gun shopping, and soon.

They wound along back roads until they reached Sunrise Ridge Lane, only two miles or so as the crow flies. It wasn't hard to find the spot of the crash. Red and blue light throbbed off trees and low lying clouds like a spotlight announcing Black Friday's midnight sale.

Val pulled to the shoulder. Leaving the key in the ignition and engine running, she turned to Grace. "I need you to stay in the car. Okay?"

"I can help."

If there was one phrase that summed up Grace's philosophy of life, that was it.

"There are a lot of trained people helping here, honey. I'm afraid the big trick for both of us is going to be staying out of their way."

She crossed arms over chest and slunk low in the seat.

"I'll find out what's going on and let you know. Keep the doors locked, all right? And only open them for people you know."

Her big eyes widened with the last warning.

Val hoped she was just being paranoid, but with Hess around, she wasn't about to take a chance, even if that meant frightening her niece. "Okay?"

Grace nodded.

With that, Val stepped out into the night air. It was warmer than it had been recent nights, part of a trend the forecasters said, but it still carried a damp chill that wormed its way into Val's bones.

She passed the black-and-white, its light bar whirling, and moved on to where the fire department's Unit One idled. A young firefighter pointing the way, she peered down the rough slope that plunged into the forest preserve.

The reflective bands crossing the sleeves, legs and torsos of the firefighters' turnout gear glowed in the emergency lights. Behind them, she could make out the crumpled bluish gleam of a car.

Tamara Wade's steel blue Volvo.

For a moment, the air seemed to condense in her lungs. Just as she feared when she heard the second call, this was no ordinary accident. It was the first move in Hess's game.

"I thought I told you to get some rest."

She knew Schneider was on his way, but the gruff tone in his voice gave her a start anyway. She turned to face him. "It was Hess, Jeff."

Bushy brows lowered over skeptical eyes. "How do you know that from up here?"

"The car. It belongs to Tamara Wade."

"His attorney?"

"He wasn't happy with her."

"Hmm. You'd think firing her would suffice."

Val nodded. The joke wasn't meant to be funny, just to lighten the intensity a little, gallows humor.

It didn't work.

The group around the car broke up and a few men started trudging back up the slope. Val recognized the tall, wiry figure and his broad shouldered partner as Baker and Caruthers from EMS. They carried their stretcher up the hill.

Empty.

And they would only do that if they'd pronounced the victim dead at the scene.

"I'll call the State Crime Lab. Looks like they're about to turn the scene over to us." She turned to walk back to the road.

"Better let me do that, Val."

She pulled up short. "Right. Sorry."

"Not necessary. You know that." He plopped a big mitt on her shoulder and gave it a pat. "You, my dear, had better start thinking about getting out of town."

Val had to agree, but she didn't follow Schneider's suggestion right away. Being on suspension, she couldn't very well sneak down to the car and take a look. All that would do was add another set of footprints to an already trampled crime scene and give her and Schneider an extra dose of explaining to do.

But that didn't mean leaving immediately was her only option. After checking on Grace, she returned to Unit One and waited for the firefighters to haul their equipment back up the ridge. To her relief, Lund was among them.

Skin pale and sweat beaded on his forehead, he looked worse than she'd ever seen him, including both times his wife had died. He stowed the large hydraulic spreading tool in the truck, then followed her to a more isolated spot behind Grace's car.

She didn't ask, just waited for him to offer up what he'd observed.

"Her mouth was sewn shut."

"Sewn?"

"Needle and thread. Yeah, that bad. Also most of her body was burned, a few cuts thrown in for good measure." He looked like he might throw up, but managed to keep it in check. "Go look for yourself."

"You didn't watch the ten o'clock news, did you?" She filled him in on her suspension. "I'm getting Grace out of town tomorrow. Visiting a friend in Chicago. You should get out of town, too."

She was just being a good police chief, trying to keep the citizens in her jurisdiction safe, but somehow the suggestion felt intimate, as if she was asking him to come with her, and she found herself looking away.

"I have the feeling I'm going to be needed here. But since you're going to Chicago, I have an idea of some side trips you might want to take."

She frowned. She was obviously missing something. "Side trips?"

"Couple cemeteries down there. Northwest of the city. Might be fun to visit."

She smiled as his meaning dawned. Jeff had said he'd do it, but now that he was acting chief, the plan had changed. "You know, that is a great suggestion."

Maybe this trip would be more than a forced vacation after all.

Dale Kasdorf saw the police car through the trees along the highway before it turned into his drive.

He knew they'd be coming.

The calls from police had begun days ago, cautious words about keeping safe, warnings of dangers to come. Little did they know, the bad things had already started. The woman at the lake. Strange movements at the dairy farm next door. The car crash tonight on Sunrise Ridge. They knew bits and pieces. But only he saw all of it happening and could put the pieces together.

Or at least enough of them to be certain he didn't want any part.

He ducked back into his house and locked the door, sliding the bolts home in three places. Immediately he made for the stairs. The wood gave a hollow thunk under his boots as he descended into the cellar. The place was cold and dank. Not a place anyone sane would stay by choice. Not a place anyone would look.

And that was the point.

He crossed to one water-stained rock wall lined with shelves of canning jars. The corn relish and tomatoes and icicle pickles had been put up by his mother, and most were still good. Every once in awhile, he'd open one as a treat. To remember her sweet face and brave smile.

The rest of his childhood, he was willing to forget.

He grabbed the right side of the wood shelves and swung them into the room and out of the way, revealing the door hidden behind.

The entrance to his bunker. To his home.

He'd set the place up to be climate controlled. The chill of winter never reached in here, nor did the basement's humidity in summer. It had its own air, pumped in from outside and filtered until it was pure. It had its own generator, so he'd always have power, even when other electricity went out. It had its own water supply pumped out of the ground beneath.

The pressure seal made a satisfying sucking sound as he pulled the door open. He stepped inside and surveyed his space.

Weapons lined the walls, everything from knives to handguns to rifles and shotguns he'd modified himself. He shut the door safely behind him and feasted his eyes on his newest addition, a Charter Arms .44 Bulldog revolver like Son of Sam used.

Sweet.

He'd inherited the decrepit farm from his parents. Inherited a lot of money, too. And he'd sunk it all into this place. The ratty old farm house on the surface that was held together with little more than duct tape and Liquid Nails was merely a cover for his real home under the ground.

This was where he lived. Where he was safe. Where he couldn't be watched. Not by cops or by killers.

And if either one came after him, this is where he'd make his stand.

Val found the road to the cemetery on her third try.

It was barely a road, really, not much more than a couple of tire ruts that turned off the highway near a small gravel quarry. The first two times they'd passed, Val had chalked it up to the quarry road. The third drive by, desperation had pushed her to turn in.

The tiny Focus dipped and bucked through ruts, snow over the hubcaps in some places. Val kept her foot steady on the gas, praying they didn't get stuck.

"Is this really a road?" Grace held onto the arm rest with one hand, the other braced on the dash.

An old metal arch of the type common on gates of ranches out west straddled the non-road, proclaiming the place the White Church Cemetery, but all Val could see on the adjacent swells and valleys were the tracks of horses in snow and the top of an indoor riding arena peeking over the crest of a hill.

"The grandparents are here, right?" Grace asked, squinting at the swirling white all around them.

"Right," Val said. "Willard and Alfreda Unger."

Alfreda Unger had four daughters. Kelly's mother and her three aunts. Kelly's mother was buried in the cemetery overlooking Lake Loyal. Val and Grace had found one aunt in the first Illinois cemetery they'd visited, a Christmas wreath on the grave, likely put there by the woman's son, to whom Olson had spoken. That left Alfreda and two aunts in this cemetery.

Here there were no wreaths, and likely no visitors, since everyone in this branch of the family was already dead. The snow was much deeper, and provided they even made it without getting stuck, it was going to take some digging.

Not that Grace cared.

As grumpy as she'd been at the prospect of leaving Lake Loyal, she seemed in her element now. Val didn't know many teenagers who would jump at the chance to go gravestone hunting with their aunts, but then most were nothing like her Grace. She had taken on the task as if it was a grand adventure. Her enthusiasm had even spread to Val. At first.

She wasn't so excited about conquering this remote tundra. "We're going to need the shovel."

"It's in the back seat."

Val drove under the gate and came to a stop near a large burgundy stone that resembled the one Lund had mentioned when he'd given her directions. Leaving the

Ford parked smack in what appeared to be the middle of the road, they got out. Having finally located her gloves in the Focus, Val pulled them on along with a hat. Similarly bundled, Grace grabbed the shovel, and they trudged to the first stone.

The name etched on granite was Jones.

"No good," Grace called over the wind. "How about that one?"

They moved down the row, reading stone after stone. The wind kicked up, skimming a sparkle of fine ice crystals over the hills like sand in a desert. Val's feet grew dank in her boots. Her cheeks stung with the cold, then settled into numbness.

She was about to give up when she spotted another burgundy stone peeking through a drift near the far corner of the cemetery. This one was smaller than the first, but wide, the kind that was used to mark more than one grave. "That could be it."

She wallowed through one drift after another, Grace right at her side. There wasn't just a little more snow here than in Lake Loyal, there was a lot. A little ironic since they were many miles to the south. It was at least fifteen degrees colder, too. By the time they reached the headstone, snow filled their boots and clung to their jeans up to their knees.

The marker itself was buried, and Grace half-wiped, half dug to clear the engraving. The names Willard and Alfreda Unger etched the granite, Kelly Ann's grandparents on her mother's side.

"We found it," Grace shouted, as if discovering gold.

Val dug the shovel into the snow in front of the stone. The drift was packed hard, and by the time she'd cleared a spot of brown grass two feet square, she could feel the exertion in her back and legs, and her hand—which had been improving a little—could no longer grip the wooden handle.

The earth in front of the stone hadn't been disturbed.

Grace held out her hand while eyeing Val's. "I'll dig."

She stuffed her hand in her pocket. "My fingers are cold. Aren't yours?"

"No, I'm good. Give me the shovel."

Grace continued down the line. One aunt had died when she was a child, and Grace found her grave next to that of her parents. She cleared off the square of earth where a body would have been buried, and they found nothing but undisturbed grass, brown and frozen.

The days were growing short. That coupled with clouds moving in brought darkness earlier than Val had anticipated. With the night, the temperature dropped even further.

To think they were missing the warming trend in Lake Loyal for this.

Val hitched her coat tighter around her neck and followed Grace to the next stone. Hollywell. Then the next. Johnston.

"Here it is," Grace called. "Another Unger."

The stone was small and gray, its carving hard to make out in the snow and dimming light.

She dipped her hand in her pocket and pulled out the small flashlight she insisted Grace keep in her glove box and directed it at the marker, revealing the name

Elizabeth Unger, the woman who was once married to Jeff Schneider.

Grace cleared more of the stone with her mitten. Liz's birthdate, the dash, and ... nothing. "No death date?"

She spun around, focusing wide eyes on Val. "Elizabeth Unger is still alive?"

Chapter
Sixteen

Of course, it wasn't that simple.

"Just because a date isn't entered on Liz Unger's tombstone doesn't mean she isn't buried here." Val explained to her niece. "All it means is someone failed to have the date carved into the stone."

Grace cleared the snow in front of the grave marker, as she had with the others, and as with the others, the earth was undisturbed. "But it's weird, right? Why wouldn't someone make sure she has a death date?"

Val could think of a lot of reasons. "She might be buried somewhere else. She could have remarried before she died and was interred with her husband. She could have had children and is buried near them. For all we know, she could have retired to Florida and was buried down there."

"So this doesn't tell us anything?"

Val gave her niece an encouraging smile. "Actually, it does. It tells us we have some investigating to do. Elizabeth Unger died in a car crash, and as luck would have it, governments all over the country keep track of a lot of things, and fatal car accidents are one of them."

They climbed back into the car. Possibilities whirled in Val's head like the whipping wind and left her just as cold. Heater switched to blast furnace, she pulled out her phone and found Harlan Runk's cell number in her directory.

He answered on the third ring. "Yup."

"Harlan? It's Val Ryker."

"Hiya, sweet cheeks. What can I do ya for?" His words slurred and soft music, voices and clattering tableware sounded in the background.

No doubt the coroner was imbibing his favorite brandy old fashioned sweets at the supper club. She hoped he was sober enough to remember what she was about to tell him. And act on it. "I need you to do something for me."

"I'll be right over."

"I'm not in Lake Loyal, Harlan, and this has to do with work."

"You're breaking my heart, honey pot. But I can't deny you anything. What do you need?"

"I need you to request some medical records and compare them to what's left of Jane Doe."

"Jane Doe's got no teeth. Without teeth, it's a long shot."

"Actually the whole thing is a long shot, Harlan. But I'm desperate."

"I like the sound of that."

She stifled a groan. "The bones have a fracture that matched a broken wrist Kelly had. Can you use that to compare?"

"I seem to remember that. Yup."

"So you'll do the comparison?"

"First thing in the morning. You've got my word, princess. Now to whom am I comparing?"

"Elizabeth Unger. She's Kelly Lund's aunt on her mother's side. If I find anything else, I'll let you know." She thanked him and hung up.

Exiting the cemetery was easier, thanks to the tire ruts they made going in and the fact that they were now headed downhill. Val took Highway 14 Southeast to Palatine, then joined 53 and blended into Interstate 290.

They'd almost reached the turnoff to Bensenville when Grace finally spoke. "I don't want to stay somewhere without you."

She hadn't yet told Grace anything about her need to dash back to Lake Loyal after what they'd found in the cemetery, but with her call to Harlan, she should have known the girl would put it together. "You'll like Jack."

"Jack?"

"Jack Daniels."

She wrinkled her nose. "Isn't that booze?"

"This Jack Daniels is a friend of mine from back when I worked for the Chicago PD. Jack is short for Jacqueline. You'll have fun, Grace. She knows a lot more about fashion than I do, and if you cooperate, maybe she'll even take you to the firing range."

Of course, first she had to make sure Jack didn't mind Grace staying with her without Val present.

The pout stayed on Grace's lips despite the prospect of buying clothes and shooting guns. "You won't remember to feed the horses."

"Good thing I hired someone to do that."

"You won't remember to feed yourself."

Val could hardly argue that point, especially after the past few days. "I'll stick a Post-It on the door so I can't miss it."

"Now you're making fun of me."

Val was exhausted, and she still had to figure out what happened to Liz Unger and—provided she found something—drive the four hours back to Lake Loyal. She didn't have the energy for this. "It's going to be tough not having you there, Grace. I know you've been keeping the place together, especially lately. But I can't deal with it unless I know you're okay."

"Who's going to make sure *you're* okay?"

Her question hit Val like a hard kick. Grace was an amazing girl, always responsible, always caring for others. She was so much like her mother, it made Val's chest hurt. "I need you to do this for me, Grace. Just for a few days."

Her niece stared straight ahead out the windshield, not answering. A mile hummed under the tires, then another.

No one could administer the silent treatment like a teenage girl.

Fine. She was angry now, but she'd get over it, and she might even have a good time. Most of all she'd be safe. That was what mattered most.

Jack's directions were precise, and Val found the house in Bensenville with little problem. Her old friend and mentor looked stylishly gorgeous as usual in a pair of gray herringbone trousers and a wrap sweater that had to be cashmere. She really was too well dressed to be a cop.

In light of Val's fashion ineptitude, it was probably a good thing she moved to the middle of Wisconsin, where the chicest outfit you could wear was green and gold on game day.

As they exchanged hugs and introductions, a tall redheaded man with a charming little boy smile stepped into the room, his gait a halting shuffle that took a lot of time and a seemingly large amount of effort. He thrust out a hand.

"This is my fiancé, Latham." Jack wasn't smiling, she was glowing.

His grip was warm and felt more vital than he looked. After they made introductions all around, Latham talked Grace into a game of rummy, leaving Val and Jack to duck into the kitchen to talk.

"What do you think of Latham?" Jack said as soon as they were out of earshot.

What could Val say? Latham's eyes lit up every time he looked in Jack's direction, something he couldn't keep from doing at every opportunity. "He's great."

"I proposed to him," Jack said. "One knee, mariachi band, the works."

That caught Val by surprise. If there was a woman less romantic than she was, it was Jack. She might dress well, but fashion was her way of projecting confidence, something essential in the old boys' club of the Chicago PD. Jack kept her emotions close to her chest, and wasn't one to get dewy-eyed over a man.

Jack smiled. "I know, I know. You can't imagine it. But I've never been this happy with anyone."

Val had to admit, between Monica and now Jack, she was feeling left out. And more than a little envious. "When are you getting married?"

"I don't know. He's recovering from a brush with botulism."

So that was the reason for the shuffling steps, the pallor to his skin.

"Do you have a guy up in the north woods?"

For the flash of a second, Val thought of Lund, then she shook the thought away. "I'm a little busy lately."

"In other words, you don't want to talk about it."

"Right."

"Fair enough."

"Jack, I have a favor to ask."

"Shoot."

"I was wondering if Grace could stay with you a few days. Without me, I mean."

"Of course she can." Jack narrowed her eyes. "Something happen with Dixon Hess since we talked?"

She filled Jack in on Tamara Wade, ending with the missing death date on Liz Unger's gravestone.

After listening to it all, Jack gave a sage-like nod. "I think I have exactly what you need." She led Val to a computer and called up a vital records database.

Val slid into the chair. "Thanks."

"I'll make some coffee."

Val had downed at least five cups by the time she found what she was looking for.

Liz Unger's death records where listed under Elizabeth Schneider, not Unger, since it appeared she and Jeff Schneider never officially divorced. She'd died ten years ago from injuries sustained in a car accident, and she was buried in the White Church cemetery in Illinois.

The only problem was that there was no police report of the fatal accident, and while the cemetery had a record of her plot, a call to the White Church Cemetery's association president confirmed she hadn't been buried there. Odd that Olson hadn't picked up on those inconsistencies when looking for information on the family, especially since Schneider had assisted him.

But that wasn't all.

Val stared at the computer screen, her heart drumming so hard she thought she might be sick. In the other room, she could hear Grace laughing above the low hum of Latham's voice. The scent of apple pie drifted on the air, Jack's mother having arrived home a short time before and insisted on baking something for Grace, along with giving her tips on how to beat Latham at rummy.

The door squeaked open, and she could feel Jack watching her. "You found something."

She didn't bother asking how Jack knew. Her old friend was a master when it came to reading body language and assembling puzzles. "Seems like I came a long way to find something that was in my own backyard."

"She died in Wisconsin."

"My home county, to be precise."

Throat dry, she stared at the part that disturbed her most ... the name of the coroner who'd signed the death certificate.

Val's head was buzzing long after she'd driven back across the Wisconsin border, known as the cheddar curtain, took the Highway 12 exit circling around Madison and Middleton, and then followed it north. The rain meteorologists had predicted pattered against the windshield, and the temperature hovered around freezing.

Not a good night for driving.

In years past, this stretch of road had been dangerous, fraught with steep twists and badly banked turns. A bypass had smoothed out the rough edges, and Val continued at a good clip. Only the occasional set of headlights pierced the darkness in the oncoming lane. A mid-sized pickup followed a little too close behind.

She'd first noticed him in Janesville. Before that, she'd been too distracted by the thoughts pinging around in her head, not that they had quieted down in the miles since.

Pete Olson, Jeff Schneider and Harlan Runk.

At least one of them was lying to her, maybe all three.

She'd been a cop long enough to know that the best of people were capable of horrible acts when caught by difficult circumstances. She just didn't want to believe men she'd worked with for the past six years framed a man for a woman's death.

Or maybe even caused it themselves.

As she approached the first turn off to Roxbury, ice started to build up at the edges of the Focus's back window, and she could feel an unstable slickness under the tires. She pulled her foot from the accelerator and let the car's momentum take her around the curve.

The headlights behind drew closer, their glare flooding her car and bouncing off the rear view into her eyes.

She tilted the mirror toward the ceiling, but between the glare and her increasingly foggy vision, for a few scary moments, she could barely see.

They'd passed town after town, dozens of chances to turn off, but he hadn't. She'd slowed enough for him to pass, but he didn't take the opportunity. The truck's driver was probably a flaming asshole who happened to be traveling the same route, but unease prickled at the back of her neck all the same.

Fields stretched on either shoulder, the stubble of corn stalks barely poking through snow. She hadn't remembered how lonely this stretch of road was, farms far between, houses non-existent. Her pulse pounded in her ears, drowning out the swish of the wipers. Ice started forming on the rubber blades, and she flicked the heater to full-on defrost.

She eased around two more bends in the highway.

The headlights followed, tightening the distance, passing each intersecting road, rolling right by the occasional driveway.

Gripping the wheel in her left hand, she groped in her coat pocket and found her phone. On an icy night like this, she doubted the county sheriff's departments or local police were lacking for things to do. She wouldn't call for help based on some vague, uneasy feeling, but she wanted to be prepared in case this was more than fatigue mixed with paranoia.

She set her phone in her lap and put both hands on the wheel, forcing herself to breathe deeply and focus on the ribbon of asphalt ahead. Taking her foot off the accelerator, she let the truck creep closer. If she could get a glimpse of the license plate in her rear view mirror, she'd have something to work with.

Only there was no front plate.

She'd heard rumor of a bill working its way through the state legislature that would make a front plate unnecessary, but she couldn't quite believe the omission was as innocent as a misinterpretation of the law. In only a few minutes, she'd reach Sauk City. She'd drive straight to the police station. No way would the driver confront her there.

River bluffs hulked ahead, dark against the glow of city lights off low clouds. Businesses sprung up on either side of the road; bars, restaurants, and roadside motels catering to summer tourists. Ahead the highway funneled onto a bridge spanning the Wisconsin River. Sauk City sparkled along the far bank.

She was almost there.

The first jolt hit above her back bumper. Her car fishtailed, skimming on ice.

Shit, shit, shit.

She counter steered, careful not to overcorrect, struggling to stay on the road.

The truck hit her from the side.

The Focus careened over the ice like a hockey puck. She steered, counter steered, but it did no good. A sign advertising canoe rentals whipped by on the right. She shuddered over the end of a guardrail to the left.

Sliding, jolting, skidding.

In slow motion, yet too fast for mind and body to react.

The tires hit the river bank. For a moment, she skated over frozen sand and ice, then water surged over the hood and the airbag exploded in her face.

Chapter
Seventeen

Lund paced across his living room and looked at the wall clock for what had to be the fiftieth time in the last minute. The roads were starting to get slick now. Every few minutes his radio would come alive with an assistance call for a fender bender in Lake Delton or a car in the ditch outside of Merrimac. He figured it was only a matter of time before he had to use his extrication skills again.

You'd think one of these days people would learn to stay off the road during ice storms. Apparently that was too much to ask.

He'd gotten half way across the floor when the next call came in. As soon as he identified it as originating from outside the district, he only half listened.

Car off the road at the Highway 12 bridge in Sauk City. Vehicle submerged.

A neon green Ford Focus.

He grabbed his coat and made for the door.

Pain throbbed in Val's nose, spreading outward to swallow her whole skull. She couldn't think. For a moment, she couldn't feel. Then she opened her eyes, and recognized the coppery taste of blood filling her mouth.

What the hell had happened?

The car's air bag hung from the center of the steering wheel, mostly deflated. The car angled nose down, slowly turning to the side, and her feet were cold.

The river.

The last few minutes came rushing back, the truck, the impact, the nosedive into cold water. She shook her head to try to clear it. Instead, another wave of pain assaulted her and tears swamped her eyes, plunging the world into watery shades of dark.

She was in a car floating downriver. Floating until the engine block inevitably dragged the car under.

She had to get out.

She swiped at her eyes with her fingers. The dash lights still worked, a green glow reflecting off the water already covering the brake pedal. Something square and dark rested against the toe of her boots, and when she saw what it was, the tears almost resumed.

Her phone.

The headlights glowed under the water. But they didn't illuminate more than a greenish swirl broken by an occasional chunk of ice. Doubtful anyone would see it from the road unless they were specifically looking.

How long would it take for someone to start the search? And how would they find her in the dark water once the electrical shorted out?

She fumbled for the door lock button. If the electrical system stopped working in the cold water, she needed a way out, then she lowered the driver's side window. It stopped half way, dash lights flickering, and all went dark.

For a moment Val didn't move.

Cold dampness and the hiss of light rain on water filled the car. No scream of sirens. No human sounds of any kind.

No one was going to arrive before the car went down. No one was going to pull her out, warm and dry. It was up to her. Fingers shaking, she found the clasp of her seat belt and released it. Taking a deep breath, she pulled the latch and shoved hard against the door.

It didn't budge.

The pressure of the water outside must be holding the door. She would have to use the window. But first, she needed to make the opening bigger.

She shoved her seat back. Turning sideways, she positioned her boots at the window, drew her knees to her chest, and kicked as hard as she could.

Once. Twice.

The glass snapped at the door line and crumbled in pebbles.

The water was creeping fast, now nearly reaching the edge of the seat. She climbed into a squat, her boots under her on the driver's seat, and peered out at the frigid water.

There was no telling how deep the river was in this area. She'd heard it was often deeper where it swirled around the supports of a bridge. Stronger and more unpredictable currents, too. She was a good swimmer, even worked as a lifeguard while attending college, but that didn't matter much when the water was cold enough to shut a body down in a matter of minutes.

She couldn't help thinking of Kelly Lund, with ice matting her hair and skin the pallor of freezer-burned chicken. Is that how she would end up? Found frozen solid on a sandbar downstream?

She scanned the lights along the bank and the bridge. When she'd skidded down the bank and into the water, she'd been upstream from the structure. Now she was on the downstream side and pulling away. Businesses and houses flanked this stretch of the river. Surely someone would have seen what happened to her. Surely someone would have noticed the bright green car carried by the current.

The water inched over the seat.

Her time to hope for rescue was over. She had to get out before she went down. She spun around and pushed head and shoulders through the window, then shimmied her hips through until she was sitting on the edge of the door. Black water swirled inches below. The shore was only thirty feet from the car, maybe forty. Even fighting the cold, she might be able to make it.

She *would* be able to make it. She had to.

Taking a deep breath, she pulled her legs through, lay back in the water and pushed off.

Cold wrapped around her, so deep it made her bones ache. She let the current sweep her downstream. Battling against it would do nothing but tire her. Instead she moved her arms and legs in a sidestroke heading across the river's flow to the bank.

Her efforts grew clumsy within seconds, shivers wracking her muscles, each movement feeling close to impossible to perform. Her teeth rattled, her breath blending with the fog.

A few strokes and her feet hit bottom. She stood and forced one step, then another. Her legs were heavy, hard to control.

She looked back toward the lights, so far away. How was she swept downstream so quickly? She kept moving, hoping she was still heading toward the riverbank, though it seemed impossible land was so far away.

Walking. Trudging. Wading through the water. One foot, then the other.

A scream reached her. Her own? No, someone else. Something else.

A siren?

She wanted to turn around again, see if help was coming, signal where she was, but it was too hard. Too much effort. She tried to speak, but her voice was garbled. Not that it mattered. No one was there to hear.

The river bank was close, so close, only a few steps. She forced her foot to move forward, then the other, then … the sandy bottom fell out beneath her.

She toppled forward. Cold swallowed her. She fought, thrashed. Shore was so close, she could almost reach out and touch the ice, the sand.

Almost.

Her clothing was so heavy, her coat and boots pulling her down, the current sweeping her downstream. Her foot hit something hard. A fallen tree in the water. Branches scratched her face, tangled in her hair.

Holding her there. Holding her down.

The sirens seemed so far away, too far to reach. She was so tired.

Too tired to think.

Too tired to feel.

Too tired to fight.

The fog pulsed red and blue.

Still blocks from the river, Lund could see the Sauk City rescue workers had already arrived. He didn't let himself think of Val, wonder where she was, if she was okay. He'd learned to compartmentalize his feelings long ago, to shove his concerns aside and do his job. Worry was the enemy of action. Worry was to sit and do nothing, and he didn't do nothing well.

The light ahead flicked to yellow.

Making sure the intersection was clear, he pressed the accelerator, increasing his speed enough to make it through without adding to the number of people who needed rescuing tonight.

The lights grew brighter the closer he came to the river. Finally he reached the bridge. A ladder truck from the Sauk Prairie fire district blocked the street, lights blazing, its bulk acting as a barricade.

He pulled his truck into a restaurant parking lot and climbed out. He would go the rest of the way on foot. Cold mist enveloped him and clung in droplets to his hair and clothes. From the look of things, the efforts were focused on the far side of the river, the direction from which Val would be traveling driving north from Chicago.

He stepped past the truck and onto the bridge. Even at this distance, he could see the responders on the river bank, shadows scurrying in front of the foggy glare of searchlights. And he could see what they were pulling from the water.

The car.

Despite his practiced cool, he could feel another swirl of adrenaline dump into his system, raising the rate of his heart a few notches, making his legs feel shaky. He forced himself to focus, remain calm, but before he realized what he was doing, he had broken into a run.

"Hey, stop!" A cop he didn't recognize shouted.

Lund kept going.

He caught a flash of one of the firefighters working in the lights near the car. Red hair and round cheeks, he looked familiar. Lund couldn't remember the guy's name to save his life, but he'd met him at some point.

He raced for the car. "Is she in there?"

The guy squinted up at him for a few seconds before recognition seemed to dawn. He shook his head. "Car's empty."

Relief released the grip on his lungs and he gasped in a breath. Then he realized if she wasn't in the car …

He stared out over the cold dark river pocked with chunks of ice.

"We got in touch with the owner, though. Her aunt was driving, and she was alone, which means …"

Alone. In the frigid water.

"… looking for one body."

He could have conjured up images of Kelly, but he didn't, forcibly pushing them from his mind. Instead, he started downstream. "Fan out. She has to be here."

"Lund—" The firefighter grabbed his arm.

He yanked away from the man's grip. "Get moving! Search, damn it! The car wasn't that far from shore. She has to be here."

He moved as quickly as he could over ice-crusted snow. To his relief, he could hear the others break into motion behind him. Lights bobbed over water and shore.

Out ahead, he was the first to spot the dark form.

He broke into a run. "I found her! Over here! I found her!"

She was face down in the water, tangled in the branches of a fallen tree. Her arms were flung out in front of her, the fingers of her left hand extended, as if trying to claw her way out of the snag.

He slid down the steep bank and plunged through the fragile edging of ice and into the water. Cold current swirled around his waist, pushing him downriver, aching in his bones.

He reached her in just a few steps. Snapping branches, he untangled her and gathered her in his arms.

She'd been so close to shore. Only a few feet, and she would have made it. Inches.

Cradling her tight to his chest, he waded to shore. The slosh of water sounded brittle as ice. He tried not to think, not to feel the stillness of her body, not to recognize what that stillness meant.

He'd failed to save Kelly.

He'd failed to save Tamara Wade.

He couldn't fail Val.

Eyes closed, she appeared to be sleeping, her face slack, not even a twitch under her lids.

He carried her up the bank and lowered her to the frozen ground. "Val. Can you hear me? Val!"

No response.

He unzipped her sopping coat and opened it. She wore a white button down underneath, soaked through. He brought his fingers to her throat. Her skin was cold and still. No movement, no pulse, and from what he could see, no breathing.

Val Ryker was dead.

A hum rose in his ears.

Muscle memory was an amazing thing. He didn't have to process, his body simply took over.

He positioned the heel of one hand on her sternum, the other on top of it. Keeping his elbows straight and shoulders square, he began steady chest compressions. He didn't have to count out the first thirty. He could feel the rhythm, the depth of compression, the amount he needed.

Hands shaking from adrenaline, he placed his palm on her forehead and gently tilted her head back. With his other hand, he lifted her chin forward to open her airway.

Lowering his face near her lips, he watched her chest, willing it to rise and fall. He listened for breath, praying for the light touch of her exhale on his skin.

Nothing.

"Hang in there, Val. For Grace. For me."

He pinched her nostrils shut, then sealed his lips over hers and blew a breath into her lungs.

Her chest rose, then fell.

He gave her another, breathing for her. Then he started the next cycle, shifting back to her chest, compressions pumping her blood through her body, taking over for her heart.

"You aren't going to die, Valerie Ryker," he commanded, voice hoarse. "I won't let you."

Chapter
Eighteen

Val remembered little of the trip in the ambulance other than sleepiness and confusion and a female EMT with the shoulders and bedside manner of a professional wrestler peeling off her clothes and ordering her not to talk.

All in all, not one of her better dates.

Now she lay in bed with warm compresses on her neck and groin and a plastic tube of oxygen with its fingers up her nose.

A rap of knuckles sounded on the door.

"Come in."

She'd been hoping it was the doctor, giving her the go ahead to check out and go home, but she couldn't hold back the smile when Lund stepped into the room.

"Hey, there."

"Hey." She remembered his voice calling her out of unconsciousness, his lips on hers, his touch warm, demanding she live.

David Lund had saved her life.

"How did you find me?" she asked.

He gave her a crooked smile. "Just lucky, I guess. How are you feeling?"

"Kinda cold."

"You should have known better than to go swimming in December."

"Live and learn."

He stepped into the room and stopped, as if unsure if he should come closer. "I'm just glad you're living. I doubt you'll ever learn."

"You might be right about that. Although I don't think you're one to talk."

"No, I guess not." The smile slipped from his lips. "I'm … I'm just glad it worked out okay."

"Thanks to you."

He shook his head. "I should have gone with you to Chicago."

When she'd left, she'd urged him to get out of town. She'd never mentioned him going with them to Chicago. But somehow the thought had been in her mind at the time. And it sounded good on his lips now. Natural.

Maybe that was what happened when someone brought you back from the dead. "Yes, you should have."

"You're just saying that so you could dump me off at your friend's house with Grace."

"You mean, where you'd be safe? If I could have, I would have."

"And you would rush back to Lake Loyal all on your own to be the blue canary?"

"Blue canary?"

"Our nickname for cops."

"Like a canary in a coal mine?"

His grin was his answer. "Cops charge in. Firefighters like to assess the situation, take a more intellectual approach."

"Cowardly, you mean." She had to match his smile. If ever there was a word that didn't describe David Lund, cowardly was it.

"No more coal mines, okay? At least not for a while?" He stepped closer.

For a moment, she thought he might take her hand in his and was surprised to realize how much she wanted him to. "How long?"

He gripped the bed rail instead. "How about until Hess is back behind bars?"

"I have to do my job."

"You're on suspension. It's not your job."

"You don't really think that's going to stop me."

"Not really, no. But he almost killed you, Val."

"The truck ... I don't think it was Hess."

His brows arched in surprise.

"Hess wants revenge."

"Ramming you off the road and into the river isn't good enough for revenge?"

"It's not personal enough. He'd want me to know it was him. He would want to look me in the eye."

"So who was it?"

She told him about the inconsistencies and missing documentation surrounding Elizabeth Unger's death. "The death records show that she died from a car wreck ten years ago, but none of the other paperwork exists. There's no accident report. The cemetery president says she was never buried there."

"And who knows what you found?"

"I called Harlan Runk around four-thirty and asked him to compare her medical records with the skeleton of Jane Doe."

"Let me guess. He was the coroner who certified her death."

"Yes." Just thinking about it made her upset all over again. She'd trusted Harlan, even liked him. She hated the idea that he might be wrapped up in something un-ethical or even illegal. She couldn't imagine it.

"You think the coroner killed her?"

She automatically shook her head. "That's a pretty big leap."

Lund nodded. "But could it be possible?"

She wanted to say no, but it was beginning to seem as if anything could be possible. "Haven't a clue. But I do know he was aware I was driving back to Lake Loyal."

"And if he falsified a death certificate for some reason, he might have motive to run you into the river."

"Right." As hard as all this was to wrap her mind around, it felt good to be able to talk about it.

Lund shifted his feet, the soles of his shoes squeaking on the waxed tile floor. "But if Jane Doe died ten years ago, and she wasn't buried, why didn't we find her un-til now?"

"Maybe she didn't die back then. Or maybe her body was hidden all that time."

Another knock and the door opened. A beanstalk of a man wearing scrubs and coke bottle glasses entered. His gait was awkward, a cross between Big Bird and Pee

Wee Herman, comparisons Val was sure would date her immediately.

"Doctor Seabrook." He thrust out a hand, first shaking Lund's then Val's. "Sorry to have to break up the party."

Lund nodded to the man and tossed her a small smile. "I'll go only as far as the cafeteria. Be back in a few."

Val nodded. Pushing thoughts of false deaths, hidden bodies and murder to the back of her mind for the moment, she reluctantly focused on her health.

Doctor Seabrook turned out to be as quick, professional and efficient as a doctor could be, save for the strong scent of wintergreen floating around him and his ice cold hands. By the end of the examination, she wondered if she had been fine all along, and he should be the one getting treatment for hypothermia.

After making several notations on her chart, he eyed her through his thick lenses. "Any medications?"

"Just birth control pills. I take them for cramping."

"Pretty severe?"

"Without them? Yes."

"Are you still taking the Gilenya?"

"Not anymore."

He frowned and peered at her over his hawk-like nose.

She knew that wouldn't go over well. But she didn't want to explain why she'd discontinued the prescription, that taking the drug was an unhappy reminder of a condition she was desperate to ignore.

Obviously she couldn't ignore it any longer.

"We're going to have to get you back on it." He made a couple more notes, ending the last with a flourish of his pen. "That should be about it. Any questions?"

"I'm just wondering … my condition … " She didn't know why it was still so hard to just come out and say the words, even to a doctor treating her, but clearly she was still clinging to any form of denial available.

His eyebrows pulled together and he looked down at the clipboard in his hands. "You're referring to the multiple sclerosis?"

There it was, floating in the air like a poisonous cloud. "How does it mix with hypothermia?"

"Hypothermia can be a complication of multiple sclerosis. It's rare but severe." The confusion lifted and he gave a shake of his head and a short chuckle. "But that's not what you're asking, is it? In your case, I'm pretty sure it was the river that did the trick."

"Will it increase symptoms?"

"Any stress on the body can increase the incidence and severity of symptoms."

That's what she figured, and she knew what was coming next. "Don't tell me, we won't know until we know."

He pressed his lips into a sympathetic line. "Everything about the disease is unpredictable. I wish I could tell you more."

"When can I leave?"

"Tonight, if you really want. But I'll need to see you tomorrow morning to get you back on the medication. Your heartbeat will have to be monitored after taking the first dose. I'll have a nurse set something up."

She nodded. With no vehicle, she'd have to ask Lund to give her a ride to a rental company. "Thanks, doctor."

"You're a lucky woman."

Funny, she didn't feel lucky. But she knew he was right. At least Lund had been at the river to find her, and Grace was safe in Chicago with Jack. "Thanks."

Dr. Seabrook turned to leave, coming to a halt in the doorway. "Looks like the party's back on. Listen, she's been through a lot. Don't tire her out."

Val eyed the door, expecting to hear Lund's answer. Instead, a young female voice familiar and dear as her own heartbeat answered with a tear-soaked promise. "I won't."

Fatigue covered Val like the river's cold water, sapping her strength, dragging her down.

She watched Grace enter the hospital room, steps tentative, eyes red around the edges.

"The doctor," her niece said. "He was talking about multiple sclerosis?"

Val's head throbbed. This couldn't be happening. Out of all the people she wanted to keep the MS secret from, the most important was Grace. "Why aren't you in Chicago?"

Grace's eyes shimmered in the fluorescent lights overhead, another flood building. "I got a call on my cell. They told me about the car, asked who was using it. I … I had to make sure you were okay."

The possibility of someone in the Sauk City PD following up on the car in the river hadn't even occurred to her. If it had, she could have called Jack, warned her, asked her to keep Grace from racing back to Wisconsin in some kind of panic. Of course, her niece had to have left Chicago hours ago, while Val was in no shape to do anything, even if she'd known about the call. "How did you get here?"

Grace stared at the floor. Grasping her hands in front of her, she picked at the cuticles of her right hand, something she'd done since she was little. During the bad times, she used to keep at it until her fingers bled.

"How did you get here, Grace?"

"I borrowed Jack's car."

"Jack's car? That old Nova?"

She nodded.

"You stole Jack's Nova?" Val brought her hand to her aching head, getting tangled in the oxygen tube on the way. Her straight-A, brainiac niece was a car thief? She had to call Jack and explain, apologize.

"I'll give it back."

"That's not the point."

"The point is that you almost died." Her voice caught, and the tears surged, spilling down her cheeks. "And … and now you have a disease?"

"Never mind that." Val glanced around the room. Her cell phone was laying somewhere on the bottom of the river or being swept on its way to the Mississippi. How in the hell was she supposed to make a call? "I need a phone."

"Why didn't you tell me you were sick? I could help you. I could take care—"

Val jolted upright in her bed. "That's exactly why I didn't tell you." She wanted to take the girl by the shoulders and shake her, make her listen. Instead she felt so shaky herself, she wasn't sure she could get out of bed without landing on her face.

"I can help."

"I don't want your help, Grace. The last thing I want is your help."

Her big blue eyes looked genuinely bruised. "Why?"

"Because *I'm* the one who's supposed to help *you*."

"But I don't need—"

"Yes, you do. You need to go to school. You need to live your life. You don't need to take care of someone who's sick. Not again."

"But Aunt Val, I love you."

Now tears brimmed her own eyes. The room rippled in front of her, white on white, Grace's distraught face a blur. "I love you, too, sweetheart. But I don't want you to worry about me. I don't want you to take care of me. You've had enough sickness in your life."

"It's not your choice what I do."

"This part? This is my choice."

Grace shook her head, her hair sticking to one wet cheek.

Val knew she had to find a way to explain, to make Grace understand, but she didn't have a clue how. "Do you know what MS is?"

"I don't know. Not really."

"It's a problem with my immune system. Those defenses my body has to fight off infection? They're attacking my nervous system. My brain, my spinal column, any of my nerves. When an attack happens, the swelling can make the nerve shut down."

Grace said nothing, and Val couldn't tell if she was following or too upset to even think about seemingly random medical details. She'd never talked to anyone outside of doctors about her disease before, and she knew her description sounded like something she'd read in a pamphlet she'd picked up in a specialist's waiting room. "Sometimes I have problems, and sometimes I feel perfectly normal."

"What kind of problems?"

This was the part she really didn't want to get into. Not only was she afraid she'd scare Grace, but there was no list she could rattle off, no definitive symptoms she could recite. "Lots of things. Almost anything. Right now, I have some numbness in my right hand."

Her narrowed eyes flew to Val's right hand. "Just numbness?"

"Mostly." Before her dip in the river, she'd thought the hand was improving. Since she'd awakened in the hospital, the fingers again felt like rubber, like something other than her own flesh. She hadn't been able to get them to move at all, not something she wanted to describe to Grace.

She decided to skip telling her niece about the spasm in her neck, too, which had also grown worse, and the hint of blurred vision on the road home that hadn't abated. "The individual symptoms aren't the important thing. MS can show up just about anywhere. But it also goes away."

"You mean it can be cured?"

"Well, not really." There was a fine line between reassuring her and outright lying. Val didn't want to lie. "But I could go years without any sign of it. I *have* gone years."

"Then just let me help you when you are having problems."

"And you're going to do what? Drop out of school to babysit me?"

Grace turned away as if Val had slapped her.

"I'm sorry, sweetheart. I don't mean to be cruel. But you have to realize, the most important thing to me is—"

"Not needing anybody. I know."

"Is that what you think?"

"Isn't it?"

"No. I need you, sweetheart. I love you. That's why the most important thing to me is you going to college, living your life how you want."

"What if what I want is to take care of you?" If she'd been a few years younger, she would have stamped her foot. "It's always like this. I want to keep the horses, so you buy a farm. I mention fashion, you take me shopping. I want to give back, too."

Val had to remember, Grace was just a kid. As smart and caring and pulled together as she seemed, she was a teenager.

And she was her mother's child.

"I didn't just develop MS out of the clear blue. It runs in our family. Your grandmother had it, too."

Her eyes sharpened, and she leaned forward.

"She was diagnosed around the time I was leaving for college, a little older than you."

"Did she tell you, at least?"

"Yes. She told me."

She pursed her lips and nodded, as if Val had just proven her point.

"And I went to college anyway. And after I graduated, I attended the police academy. I went home during breaks, visited. I saw her getting worse over the years, but I never moved back home. I didn't give up my life to take care of her."

"And you think you did the right thing?"

Val had to answer honestly, and it was perhaps the hardest word she'd ever uttered. "No."

Grace stared at her a long time without speaking. When she did open her mouth, her voice was a whispered plea. "Then why do you want that for me?"

"I didn't stay home. I didn't watch my mother's body stop working. I didn't take care of her on the days she couldn't walk or couldn't see or couldn't speak. I wasn't with her when she finally died. Your mom did all that, Grace."

A minute ticked by, maybe two.

A phone rang at the nurses' station. Rubber-soled shoes squeaked on waxed floors. A machine beeped out a steady rhythm next door.

Finally Val managed to clear the thickness in her throat and summon the strength to go on. "Melissa never lived her life. She never went to college. She never got to enjoy parties and dating and dreaming about her future. I think when she met your dad, she just wanted to be normal so desperately, wanted to have a romance, wanted to fall in love …"

"And he was married." She didn't say the words with bitterness, but as fact.

Val had never met Grace's dad, but unlike Grace, she *did* judge. He'd taken advantage of her sister, played around with her, then went his merry way. The only thing she couldn't hate him for was the baby he'd left behind.

"But she got to have you. To keep you. After you were born, she was so happy. It was the happiest I'd ever seen her."

The corners of Grace's mouth turned up a touch, then the smile fell away as she remembered the rest. The part Val didn't have to tell her, because she was there.

More there than Val.

And that was the bottom line, wasn't it?

"You've already had to spend so many years of your life taking care of your mom. I won't have you spend more of them hovering over me."

"But you're … you're all I have, Aunt Val. I want to help."

Val shook her head. "I owe her, Grace. I took from her. I won't take from you."

"And buying a farm so I could keep my horses, is that paying her back?"

"I did that just because I wanted to." Val gave her niece a heartfelt smile. "I always wanted horses, too. Didn't I ever tell you that?"

Grace's frown deepened. "I'm serious."

"I am, too. I'd give you everything in the world, Grace, if I could. What I can give you is a place to keep your horses, an education for your brilliant mind, and freedom to live your life without taking responsibility for me."

She swallowed into an aching throat, her eyesight not only blurred by the MS, but by tears. "I want to see you blossom the way your mom never could."

Chapter
Nineteen

Monica really hadn't had that much to drink, but the beeping of the slots, the jingle of a jackpot of tokens pouring from the machine, and the hormonal buzz she felt whenever she was around Derrick must have intensified the booze content of the casino's cocktails.

She leaned against the solid strength of her man, the brightly patterned carpet swirling in front of her. "Whoever is tending bar tonight makes some kind of strong whiskey sours."

Scooping the latest haul of tokens into his plastic cup, Derrick grinned.

Monica melted.

He might not be George Clooney handsome, but that didn't matter to her. Hair was overrated. So was a washboard gut. What Derrick had was more special. Whenever he looked at her—like his grin now or a glance across the room or gazing deep into her eyes while they were making love—she always felt he wasn't seeing her as she was, flaws and all, he was seeing the woman she wanted to be.

Another gambler bumped into her from behind.

She staggered forward, and Derrick wrapped an arm around her, keeping her on her feet.

Normally she'd be pissed. She might even spin around and lecture the stranger on watching where he was walking. Tonight she appreciated the gentle shove closer to Derrick's side.

"You okay?" her prince asked.

"I'm thinking I'd like to go back to the room."

"I've never known you to tire out quite so early."

"I'm drunk, honey. I never said I was tired."

That little twinkle she loved lit his eyes. "So you don't want to go to bed, Monica?"

"Bed? Sure. Or maybe floor or shower or whirlpool tub. Hell, maybe we won't even make it to the room." She moved her hand down to his crotch and gave him a little feel.

He didn't have to tell her he liked the way she was thinking, she could see his excitement in his face … and feel it stir in her palm.

They made it to the elevator. As soon as the door closed behind them, they were kissing like teens. Derrick skimmed his hands under her sweater, unhooked her bra and had her bare breasts in his hands before the car started its ascent.

Okay, so a little more efficient than any teen.

Monica had his belt open, fly down and was just pulling him out when the bell chimed. Giggling, she pulled her sweater down and he attempted to cover himself with his shirt tail as the door slid open. He didn't succeed.

Luckily the corridor was clear.

She sagged against the wall, trying to catch her breath. "Let's make a run for it."

"My shirt's stuck in the zipper," Derrick said, his words slurring, too.

Monica couldn't contain her laughter.

"Hey, it's all your fault."

They laughed all the way down the long hall. Derrick was still trying to adjust himself when they reached the room, and he was still failing.

"Don't bother. We'll be inside in a second." Monica dipped her hand into the back pocket of her jeans for the key card.

The pocket was empty. "Where'd I put it?"

"It's right here." Derrick turned to the side, his shirt doing nothing to hide him.

Another wave of laugher took Monica. "'The key card, Derrick. Please. I must have left it in the casino or something."

"Should I go down like this and look for it?"

She had to get him inside, but not with the intention of covering him up. "I think you should just use your key and let us into the room, so I can take care of that problem for you."

"Deal." He pulled a card from his pocket, and they stumbled into the room.

Monica pulled her sweater and bra over her head. Her jeans and panties came next. She left them in a heap on the floor and perched on the edge of the bed naked.

Derrick had gotten his shirt off, but was having a tough time getting his shirt tail unstuck from the zipper.

Of course, he had an exuberant obstacle in the way.

"Come on over here." The room felt like it was sway-ing, like a small boat on a rough sea. How in the world did they manage to drink so much? Any minute she might fall over in a naked heap. But even though she knew she'd have one hell of a hangover tomorrow, she wasn't going to pass up the opportunity for wild, drunken, monkey sex tonight, if she could possibly stay upright for it.

Or even if she couldn't. "Let me do that for you, baby. I'll rip it out with my teeth."

Grinning Derrick staggered toward her and stepped between her open thighs. She'd just taken him deep into her mouth when she saw movement out of the corner of her eye.

"Have to admit, I wasn't sure what I was going to do to you, but inspiration strikes at unexpected times."

She turned in the direction of the voice and stared into the eyes of Dixon Hess.

Chapter
Twenty

When Lund got back to Val's room, he was more than a little surprised to see Grace perched awkwardly in a chair next to her bed. "Hi, Grace."

"Hi."

He shot Val a questioning look.

She answered by holding out her hand. "Can I use your cell phone?"

He handed it to her.

Her conversation was brief, and while she talked, he tried to coax a little information out of her niece. "So you heard about your aunt's accident?"

"That's why I came back. I had to make sure she was okay."

Good kid. He would imagine some nieces might be concerned about having their car submerged in a river, but apparently that wasn't anywhere near the top of Grace's mind.

Hours had passed since he'd found Val in the Wisconsin River, but it would have taken a good chunk of time for Grace to make the drive, especially on treacherous roads.

She must have found out about the accident almost immediately. "How did you get here so quickly?"

"The police called me about the car."

"And you flew up here? Or did you just beam yourself?"

The girl didn't crack a smile. She also didn't answer.

"She stole my friend's car." Val handed him back his phone.

"Didn't see that one coming."

Val eyed Grace. "Why don't you run down to the vending machine, sweetheart? You must be starving."

The girl's eyes filled with tears. "I really am sorry I took the car. I didn't know what else to do, and I didn't want you to be all alone."

"I know." Val seemed exhausted.

Understandable under her circumstances, but Lund got the feeling he'd missed more than the revelation that Grace had stolen a car. Once Grace left to plug the machines for food, he'd find out what. He dug into his pockets and pulled out a few dollars and some change. "Do you have cash for the machines?"

Grace nodded, but he slipped a few bills into her hand anyway. Thanking him, she scampered from the room. And he turned his full attention to Val. "Everything okay?"

"Jack said she would have put out an APB for the Nova, except she was secretly hoping not to get it back."

"I'm not talking about the car."

"Grace? No, she's decided she's going to take care of me."

He was only starting to get to know Val on a personal level, but he could still imagine how well that went over.

"Did you tell her you have a policy against accepting too much help?"

"Something like that."

"Anything else?"

She stared up at the ceiling.

"You don't want to tell me."

"Don't take it personally. I'm not much of a sharer."

"Hmm. Mysterious."

She shook her head. "Not really. Everyone has certain tender subjects. Things no one else knows."

"Not if you've been investigated for murder."

She tilted her head to look at him. "I hope you understand about that. It's my job."

"I understand." Funny thing was, he no longer cared that she knew his secrets. He'd probably spill all of it willingly now, if she asked. A feeling she obviously didn't share. "If you want to talk sometime, though, I'm here."

She watched him for a long time. Finally she offered a little smile. "I appreciate that."

"But you won't take me up on it? You won't tell me what you need?"

"Not now, no."

"Ever?"

"We'll see."

He let quiet settle over the room. Val Ryker intrigued him, he couldn't lie. She was sexy and smart and a force to be reckoned with. But he got the sense she also needed something—help, support—whether she would fess up to it or not.

He couldn't shake the feeling that getting to know her carried a risk, a challenge. And God knew, he was a sucker for that particular adrenaline rush.

"I'll let you get some sleep." He turned to leave.

"I'll tell you one thing I need, Lund."

He stopped and turned back, pleased she hadn't let him walk out the door. "What's that?"

"I need to go to Baraboo."

"To talk to the coroner?"

"I have to know what's going on. I've known Harlan for a long time. I have to give him a chance to explain."

"Right now? Dressed like that?" He raised his brows at her backless gown.

"The doctor said I can leave, but I'm having some tests done tomorrow morning. I don't want Grace to stay at the hospital all night. She needs sleep. It's been a rough few days."

"And not just for Grace." The first time he'd been in her room, he'd wanted to touch her, but he'd stopped short. This time he crossed to her bed and clasped her right hand in his. "What do you need, Val? Just you?"

He squeezed her fingers.

She didn't squeeze back.

Seconds ticked by before she finally spoke. "I would absolutely kill for a hot shower."

Not exactly what he was hoping for, but he was a patient man … at least about some things. "How about Grace and I go buy you some clothing that's not soaked with river water, and then you check out of the hospital and into a hotel in town for the night? Then you can have your shower, and Grace can have her sleep, and you can be back first thing in the morning."

"And what will you have?"

"An adjoining room … and the knowledge that I was allowed to help the woman who doesn't believe in accepting any."

"You think I'll go along with it?"

"I hope so. After your tests, we'll drive to Baraboo."

"You have it all figured out, don't you?"

He just smiled. "Not even close. But I'm willing to try."

Checked into a hotel near the hospital, Val didn't get her hot shower. Instead she settled for a warmish spray, afraid the heat might make her symptoms worse. But the experience was rejuvenating all the same. River water odor replaced by shampoo and conditioner that smelled like spring flowers, she wrapped her head in one towel and her body in another.

When she emerged from the bathroom, Grace was asleep. Val pulled the blankets over her niece and soaked in the peaceful expression on her face. If there was anything on earth more precious than the face of a slumbering child, Val had never witnessed it. Even though Grace was now a teenager, when her eyes were closed and her breathing steady, Val could still see that little girl with a missing front tooth who believed the world was good and that everything would turn out all right.

What Val wouldn't give for both Grace and her to feel that way again.

She glanced at the door that led into Lund's room. He'd explained to Grace that he'd arranged for adjoining rooms so he could make sure she and Val were safe. Val was sure that was part of it, but she also recognized the rest.

The invitation.

When he'd finally held her hand in the hospital, she hadn't been able to feel it. She wanted to feel his touch now. She wanted to fill herself with his warmth.

She wanted him to make her believe everything would be okay, if only for a little while.

There were many reasons to stay in their room, to curl up under her own covers and sleep, but she didn't want to think about any of those now. The past days had been hell. Just in the past few hours, she'd died and come back to life, she'd had to confess her biggest secret to the one it would hurt most, and she'd had to face, once again, her sister's sad life and her own role in the way it had played out.

She didn't know if she was ready for whatever seemed to be growing between her and Lund, she wasn't even sure she wanted it to grow, but whatever happened, she couldn't live with not knowing.

She couldn't live with never feeling his touch.

She'd read that the adrenaline of life-and-death encounters could stoke the libido, and she supposed that was what she was feeling now. But even knowing where this desire came from wasn't enough to make her do the sensible thing. She'd almost died. Technically, she had. And now more than anything, she needed to feel alive.

She stepped to the door, slid the dead bolt free, and pulled it wide.

Lund's side of the double doors was open, just as he'd said it would be. He was sitting on the bed watching TV. He looked up at her and reached for the remote. "Hi."

"Hi." When she'd first thought about going to him, while standing in the shower's spray, she'd envisioned dramatically dropping her towel and climbing onto the bed, sexy and bold. Instead she just stood there, uncertain what to do next.

He slung his long legs off the side of the bed, pulled her into the room, and closed the door. He unwrapped her hair first, wet waves falling to her shoulders. Then he slipped the towel off her body.

Her throat felt dry.

His gaze skimmed over her breasts, her belly, her legs. A smile played at the corners of his lips, and he reached for her and buried his face in her hair. "You're beautiful."

His whisper tickled her ear, and warmth spread over her skin.

He skimmed his hand up her body, over her breast, as if touching something priceless. He kissed along her cheekbone, then took her lips.

His kiss was tender at first, then grew in intensity. He cupped a hand behind her head, holding her to him as if he couldn't quite get close enough.

It had been so long since she'd lost herself in a kiss, so long since she'd felt herself opening like this.

She'd kissed him too long, she was sure. His hands moved over her, caressing her breast, kneading her buttocks, slipping between her legs. And she just let him. Selfish. Never wanting him to stop.

He steered her to the bed, never taking his lips from hers, his tongue exploring, finding, delighting.

Arms around her, he lowered her to the mattress and started moving down her body, kissing, licking, nipping, until he centered himself between her legs.

He was still fully clothed, but she just lay there, letting him taste her, letting the sensations build and crash, build and crash. Chills rose over her skin, only to be chased away by heat. Spirals of light exploded behind her eyes. Her body clenched in ecstasy and relaxed in pleasure.

She wasn't sure how long they'd been together like this when she finally found the strength to reach for him. "I'm sorry."

He rose, his lips glistening with her, then moved up her body. "Sorry? Why sorry?"

"Your clothes." She started at his buttons with her left hand. "I didn't even undress you."

"That's what you're worried about?" He pushed up from the bed and shucked his shirt, jeans and underwear. "Better?"

She let herself look at him, the muscle of his chest and belly, the light sprinkle of hair trailing to his erection.

"See? It's not as if I haven't been enjoying myself, Val."

She nodded at the sight of him. "I'm glad."

He knelt on the bed beside her. "You never have to be sorry, not with me. You just have to promise to enjoy yourself, too. And know that you deserve it. You think you can handle that?"

It was a good question, one she wasn't sure she could answer, but she was damn well going to try.

She curled her fingers around him. "Yeah, I think I can."

Irena liked her job. Most days. Unfortunately today was not one of them.

It started with the drunk who had thrown up next to the elevators after gorging on the breakfast buffet. Things had grown worse when she found herself stuck cleaning the honeymoon suite all on her own and no one had told her that instead of a honeymoon, it had been used for a bachelor party. And to end her shift, there was a terrible smell coming from room 811.

Tips had been down lately, too. And while she never relied much on them, most weeks she could make grocery money. If this kept up, she'd be lucky if she could buy a pack of gum in the hotel's overly expensive gift shop.

She restocked the stack of plastic cups and packets of coffee, then giving the room a once over, she headed out the door and pushed her cart to the last room on her list.

811.

She picked up that strange stink when she was still two rooms away.

Why did staying at a hotel make some people act like animals? She swore to God it smelled like someone had taken the nastiest shit ever and not in the toilet.

Dreading what she might have to clean up next, she stopped the cart close enough to the wall for people to walk around and started counting out how many towels and toilet paper rolls she had left.

Should be enough.

Next she moved to coffee and sugar packets. When she had nothing left to count, she grabbed an armload of towels, took one last deep breath, and knocked on the door. "Maid service. Clean your room?"

She listened for a beat.

No answer.

"Maid Service."

When silence answered again, she grabbed the pass-key hanging from the lanyard around her neck, swiped it in the lock and pushed the door open.

The smell was overwhelming inside. Not just shit, but something else, something that turned her stomach. The bathroom and kitchenette area just inside the door looked respectable. Messy, coffee and cups needing re-stocking, but not dirty in the least. The mini fridge was working and empty, nothing rotting inside that could explain the stomach-turning smell.

It wasn't until she stepped further into the room that she found the answer, smack in the middle of the king-size bed.

Two naked and mutilated corpses lay on the blood-soaked duvet, staring at her, duct tape sealing their mouths.

Chapter
Twenty-One

After a night of sleep and a morning of sitting around the hospital, Val was feeling rested. Of course, rest and medication weren't the only reasons for that. More likely, her night with Lund was to thank.

She was grateful they hadn't had time to talk things over. She wouldn't have known what to say. When she was diagnosed, she'd vowed never to allow herself to be a burden, not on Grace and not on a man. And of all the men in the world, Lund would be just the one to not only accept that role, but encourage it.

She wasn't sure she could go there.

So she'd told him she had to get back to her own bed before Grace woke, then she'd returned to her side of the double door and replaced the scent and feel of his skin in reality with that in her dreams. And now she had only the whisker burn on her cheeks and soreness between her thighs to remind her.

She peered at Lund's pickup in the Nova's rear view mirror.

If truth be told, she liked seeing him there, knowing he was with her. She was also grateful she and her niece wouldn't have to confront Harlan alone. While she had trouble thinking of him as dangerous, someone other than Hess had run her off the road last night, and the only one who knew she'd be on the highway was the coroner.

The roads had gotten worse since last night, and a fine drizzle was still falling, promising more to come. Salt trucks trundled along highways non-stop, spraying and spreading in a failing effort to keep up.

They passed the old Badger Ammunitions complex's miles and miles of half demolished barracks, ammunition factories and testing facilities, ice sparkling on barbed wire. Jack's Nova struggled up the steep curves flanking Devil's Lake State Park, and Val decided it was an even better idea Lund had followed, because he'd probably have to push.

They finally crested the hill on their own and passed the turn off to Lund's house. She'd been to his cozy little cabin back when he'd been a suspect the first time Kelly died. Heavily wooded, the area was beautiful every day of the year, but the addition of ice made it stunning. Each twig of oak and birch or needle of pine appeared polished and etched like sculptures of fine, frosted glass.

She had to wonder what it would be like to wake up to a sunny morning in his little cabin, a cascade of beauty outside, a warm and intimate scene within. A nice dream that could never come true.

Thoughts of Kelly's baby wound their way into her mind. She probably should have told him, but just because she was suspended didn't mean she was free of responsibility to the job.

She would check in with Becca, see if she'd learned anything in her canvass of hospitals. And then she would find a moment to break the news to Lund. Right now she had to focus on the icy road and how she was going to get the truth out of Harlan.

Even with the Nova chugging along at the speed of a go cart, they soon reached Baraboo. Harlan's ridiculous old hearse was parked in the lot, a coat of ice covering every inch. She parked the Nova next to it. They made a nice couple.

As always, Harlan was eating when they entered, though thankfully he was sitting at his computer and not hunkered over a corpse. He looked up. "Hey, sweet cheeks," he said with a mouth full of either baked beans or bot fly larvae. "You got my message?"

"Message?"

"I got ahold of those medical records you wanted this morning. I left a message on your cell."

"Phone died last night. Fell in some water." Val watched his eyes for any flicker that might signal he knew about her late night swim.

"Ahh, I knew it."

"Knew what?"

"You and me." He pointed his first two fingers to her eyes then his. "We're on the same wavelength, probably soul mates. I need to show you something, and here you are."

"Here I am." Val coaxed a smile to her lips. Whatever Harlan had found, she needed to see it while he was still in the mood to share. Grilling him about Liz Unger's death certificate could wait, at least a few minutes.

"It smells funny in here," Grace said, stepping tentatively into the room. Lund followed.

"Who's this pretty young thing with you?"

Val shook her head. Of course, Harlan didn't even see Lund, but stood at attention the minute Grace walked in. "Grace is my niece."

"I should have known. Pretty and blond must run in the family."

"She's sixteen," she said pointedly. "And this is David Lund. He's with the fire department."

Lund rated only a curt nod.

"I don't feel so well," Grace mumbled.

"Want something to eat?" Harlan lifted a spoon full of beans.

As if that would help.

"Is there somewhere Grace could sit, Harlan?" Val asked. "Somewhere she can get away from the smell?"

"The smell?" His bushy brows pulled together, as if he was genuinely confused.

"Some of us have squeamish stomachs."

"Oh, that smell." Harlan smiled. "I have the best place. Follow me."

He set down his beans and led them through a short hallway and into an office. The space was so small it could barely fit a desk and copy machine, but dominating an entire corner was a video game straight out of the eighties; Ms. Pac Man.

Harlan gestured to the game with a dramatic wave of one arm. "Wanna play?"

"Can I?"

"A pretty girl like you? You can do anything."

Val suppressed her urge to glance at Lund and give an eye roll. Once Grace got started on the game, they returned to the autopsy suite. Instead of pulling out the grisly collection of bones Val had feared, Harlan went right to the light box. He switched it on and clipped two x-rays into place. The ghostly outlines of bones showed on the screen.

"Now, these are the ulna and the radius, which would be the forearm bones to you and me."

Val recognized the images as x-rays of Jane Doe's scorched bones. She'd spent hours staring at them as well as studying the actual remains.

"I want you to look right here, at the wrist end of the bones." Harlan turned with a flourish and beamed, as if whatever it was he saw was plain as day to everyone else.

Lund asked the question first. "What is it that we're seeing?"

Harlan tilted his head slightly, peering at Lund as if a third eye had suddenly popped out in the middle of his forehead like a pimple on a teenager. "The thickening."

"From a broken wrist." Val supplied. "Kelly had one. It was an additional reason we thought the bones in the burning barrel were hers."

Lund stepped closer to the light box. "And what does this tell us?"

"Nothing," Harlan said.

"Nothing?" Lund repeated.

"How can we get it to tell us something?" Val asked, throwing in a little smile.

Harlan was always motivated by feminine smiles, and this time was no different. "Come over here."

He led them three steps to the side and pointed at the computer monitor he'd been studying when they'd entered.

Another x-ray glowed on the screen, this one with its hand still attached.

"It looks like the same injury," Lund said.

Harlan jolted upright. "Very good. I might decide to like you after all."

Val cut right to it. "Is this Elizabeth Unger that we're comparing to the Jane Doe x-rays?"

He glanced at Lund, and then focused on Val. "It most certainly is. She was admitted to the hospital when she was in her early twenties. These are the pictures from that visit."

Val and Lund exchanged glances.

"So what do you think?" Harlan asked.

"It's a good piece of evidence, but it's not enough for an ID." After all, they'd used that same injury as proof the body was Kelly's.

"I beg to differ." Harlan puffed out his chest, as if he was highly offended, then shot Val a little wink.

She had to admit, the more time she spent with Harlan this morning, the less she could imagine him running her off the road last night, not that it hadn't been a stretch in the first place. But now? It just wasn't possible. "Okay Harlan, spit it out. What are you holding back?"

He nearly danced over to the light box—an odd experience to witness—and clipped up another x-ray, this of a lower leg missing its foot. "Jane Doe again. The site of a similar injury."

Lund took a step closer. "She broke her leg, too?"

"Since it's right at the point where the bone shattered in the fire, it's hard to see unless you're looking for it. This time, I was."

He held up an index finger, pranced back to the computer, called up an x-ray of a leg, and pointed out a thickening in the same spot. "Elizabeth Unger and Jane Doe both have two bones with breaks in exactly the same place. I'd say that narrows things down quite a bit."

"Yeah," Val said. She felt sick, and still more than a little confused. "Whoever did her autopsy should have recognized those injuries as suspicious, right? He should have noted them."

His bushy gray brows lowered. "I'm not following, sweetie pie. I'm noting them right now."

"I found Elizabeth Unger's death records. Or should I say, Elizabeth Unger Schneider?"

His expression didn't change.

She continued. "She died here in a car wreck, ten years ago. She was supposed to be buried in Illinois, but her body was never interred there."

"That seems strange."

"It's not the strangest part, Harlan. Do you want to know who signed off on those records and made them official?"

He didn't hesitate. "Who?"

"You."

His brows lowered further, and he shook his head.

"You signed them, Harlan."

"What? No, I didn't."

"I saw them. I would have copies, but someone tried to kill me last night, and I ended up in the Wisconsin River."

"What?"

"Where were you last night?" Lund asked.

Harlan shook his head, paced a few steps, and shook his head again. "I heard Liz Unger was dead. I remember because she was married to Jeff Schneider years ago. But I never performed her autopsy. I may be an old fart, but I still have my memory. I never signed off on her death. And trying to kill you, honey?"

"Where were you?" Val prodded.

"At the supper club. I talked to you. Then I went home. You can ask my neighbor. We were both out salting our driveways about ten. I can't believe—"

The intercom buzzed.

"I have to see what this is," Harlan said. "Be right back."

The moment he left the room, Lund turned to Val. "What do you think?"

She let out a breath, a mix of relief and frustration. "That he's telling the truth."

"That's what I think, too. So how did his signature get on the records you saw?"

"Forged. Or maybe he signed something without really looking at what it was." She'd seen him hurry through paperwork more than once, scribbling his name without paying much attention to the forms he signed.

"So that leaves Schneider?"

"And my sergeant, Pete Olson. He was in charge of following up on Kelly's family. I'm having a hard time believing he never thought it necessary to dig a little farther into the inconsistencies surrounding Liz Unger."

"When it comes to situations like these, some people just don't want to know," Lund said.

She stared at the x-rays on the computer. "Do you think he abused her?"

"Schneider?"

She nodded.

"I don't know. I remember at least one of Kelly's aunts lived with them for a while. The abuse could have come from Kelly's father. That family ... there were a lot of skeletons in those closets."

"Maybe. But it would have been tough for anyone to fake death records ... except a police chief who knows how to distract the coroner."

Harlan rounded the corner, his face as gray as his hair. At first Val thought he overheard. Then he opened his mouth. "It's Monica Forbes. She's dead."

Chapter
Twenty-Two

Val wasn't sure she'd be welcome at the scene, but as soon as she arrived at the casino hotel, an FBI agent escorted Grace, Lund and her into the attached casino's security office and asked them to take a seat in front of one of the monitors.

The agent was clean cut in that button-down FBI agent sort of way. Hair almost black, he was a few inches shorter than Lund, but looked fit and efficient in his dark suit. He introduced himself as Special Agent Subera and got down to business. "We recovered this about five minutes ago."

Val was still shaking from the bomb Harlan had dropped in the morgue. She couldn't believe Monica was dead, couldn't wrap her mind around it. And as much as she wanted to help the FBI, who shared jurisdiction with the tribe owning the casino, she didn't know how she would handle seeing her friend's body.

And she knew she didn't want Grace witnessing it. "What's on the video?"

Agent Subera glanced at Grace. "Security footage from inside the casino. I just need you to tell me if you recognize anyone."

"Okay."

He tapped a few keys and the monitor flicked to life.

The shot showed three rows of slot machines, a handful of people scattered among them, trying their luck. She scanned the grainy image of each face, squinting her right eye in an effort to adjust to the blurring that seemed to be growing worse.

The first three people, she didn't know. Then she spotted Monica beaming as Derrick hit a button and the machine paid out. She looked so happy, her gestures exaggerated as if she was quite drunk. Derrick, too, seemed to be swaying a little on his feet.

Val's throat closed and tears welled in her eyes. She took a couple of breaths through her mouth, did her best to blink her vision clear, and pointed at the screen. "There. That's Monica and that's her fiancé Derrick."

Subera nodded as if she'd just told him what he already knew.

So it was true then. Monica was dead. Derrick was dead. And Val had a feeling she knew who did it.

As if conjured by her thoughts, Dixon Hess walked down the aisle toward the couple, watching the row of machines as if trying to pick the best one to play.

Val held her breath, waiting to see what he'd do.

He bumped into Monica, grabbed her a little to keep her from tipping both herself and Derrick onto the floor, and then he resumed his walk, moving off the bottom edge of the monitor.

"That was him. Dixon Hess. He bumped into them."

S.A. Subera moved the video back a few seconds and played it again, asking her to point Hess out on the screen. Then he let the footage roll.

There wasn't much left. Monica and Derrick hugged and horsed around for a few seconds, then left the frame in the direction Hess had.

"He picked her pocket," Lund said simply.

Val had to agree. "She didn't have a purse with her, so she must have had her wallet there.

"Wallet was in the room."

"Of course," she said. "It was her key."

Again Subera nodded, as if he'd already figured it out.

Val continued. "He saw they were drunk, so he grabbed the key and waited for them."

"Not drunk," said the agent. "Another camera shows him hanging out at the bar area."

"He put something in their drinks."

"We'll have to see what the tox screen finds."

Again a wave of emotion washed over her, and she struggled to hold it together. In normal circumstances, she'd ask to see the crime scene, even though she had no cause for the FBI to grant her that wish. Today, she was certain she couldn't handle seeing Monica's face without dissolving into a sobbing heap.

But there was one thing she had to know.

"Did he do anything to the bodies?"

"What do you mean?"

"Like sew their mouths shut? Something unusual?" She could feel Lund watching her, no doubt remembering what Hess had done to Tamara Wade.

"As a matter of fact, he did."

She scooped in a deep breath, as if she was about to plunge under water. "What?"

Subera glanced at Grace. "That information is restricted to law enforcement personnel."

Val nodded. "Grace, will you step right outside the door?"

Eyes looking a little shell shocked, she nodded and scampered out, more eager to escape the horror than curious for maybe the first time in her life.

Lund scooched back his chair. "You want me to leave, too?"

"Please."

Once Val and the special agent were alone, she turned to face him and braced herself. "What did he do?"

"He cut off the male's penis."

Val frowned. She didn't understand. Derrick wasn't part of the trial. He had nothing to do with Hess's conviction. In fact, Monica and he hadn't started dating until after Hess was behind bars.

So why would he mutilate Derrick in that way?

"Did he mutilate both of them?"

"She has some cuts. They looked largely superficial, though. Meant to cause pain."

"How did she die?"

"He put duct tape on both their mouths. The male has his throat cut. From what we can tell without an autopsy, it looks like the female might have choked to death."

"He choked her?"

"No. He taped something in her mouth. She aspirated her own vomit."

She almost asked what Hess had taped inside Monica's mouth, but then she knew.

Hess hadn't mutilated Derrick for anything Derrick had done. He'd done it so he could take from Monica what she loved best.

And a part of what she loved best was what killed her.

Someone was camping on an icy night like this?

Kasdorf picked up his pace, moving through evergreen and birch, pine needles cushioning his steps. He'd been out doing his usual rounds, walking the perimeter, checking to see if the trees were suffering damage from the ice storm, keeping an eye out like he always did.

The sun was going down, not that you could see it through the thick clouds. But soon it would be dark. He wanted to make sure his land was secure before night set in.

Then he smelled the smoke.

He could just imagine what was going on. Not campers, not on a night like this. So who was it? Cops? Soldiers after his arsenal? Criminals waiting until they thought he couldn't defend himself?

He had some news for them. Dale Kasdorf could always defend himself.

All he had to do was reach his bunker.

A hundred meters from his house, he picked up the tread of work boots in the snow.

Whoever it was hadn't gone to any lengths to hide his tracks, just as he hadn't seemed to give a thought to concealing the smoke.

He could hear the fire crackle, and judging from the glow on the other side of a stand of pine, he was drawing near. His hands trembled with the surge of adrenaline, but he was ready. He was capable of killing a man to defend himself and his property. Hell, he'd take on police, the IRS, even the CIA if he had to. A man's home was his castle. A man's guns were his life.

He fought through the last thicket of brush and trees. For a moment, he froze in his tracks.

His house. The flames, the smoke, they were coming from his house.

And looking up at the bonfire, smiling, was Dixon Hess himself.

Kasdorf raised his Bulldog to fire, but by the time he brought the weapon up, the bastard was gone, ducking behind trees.

Kasdorf had a choice. He could give chase or he could protect his arsenal.

Slipping the revolver back into its holster, he raced into the flames.

Chapter
Twenty-Three

Lund hated to interrupt, but when a call went out for a fire at a property near the dairy farm, he didn't have much choice, especially in light of who the owner of that property was.

The door to the security office swung open and Special Agent Subera stuck out his head. "What is it."

"I need to talk to Chief Ryker."

"It'll have to wait."

He rested his hand on the door. "Can't wait. It's about a fire. You might want to hear about this, too, if you're serious about solving your double murder."

"It's connected?"

"I'm pretty sure. Yes."

Subera swung the door wide. "Come in then."

Val stood up as he stepped inside. "What is it?"

"Fire. Kasdorf's place."

"Hess. Has to be."

Subera looked from one to the other. "Fill me in."

Lund let Val do the honors.

"Kasdorf was a witness in Monica's case against Hess."

He blew a breath through tight lips, just short of a whistle. "He's taking out everyone involved in the case?"

Val nodded. "One by one."

"Who's left?"

Lund pointed to Val, then himself. "You're looking at 'em."

"And possibly Sergeant Olson," Val added.

"But if you don't mind, I'll leave you two to talk about that. I have to someplace to be." He spun for the door.

"Wait." Val's voice.

He turned back.

"Kasdorf. The guy has an arsenal. I wouldn't be surprised if he had some really crazy stuff. You might just want to let this one burn itself out."

He saw what she was getting at. "But it would be a blast to be able to put it out myself."

She shook her head.

He held up his hands. "Kidding."

"Just be careful."

A warm feeling seated itself in his chest, right next to the tremble of worry for her. "You, too."

Val would give almost anything to take Grace and Lund, hole up in a luxury resort somewhere far away and sleep until her body functioned again and the grief she felt over Monica's death faded away. Instead she did the only thing she could.

The job … whether she was suspended or not.

Monica's murder was out of her hands. She could assist on the case, even offer herself as a witness to Hess's vendetta. But the crime didn't take place in her jurisdiction. That particular arrangement would be worked out between tribal police and the FBI.

However Liz Unger's death was something she could pursue and she intended to do just that.

Driving back to Lake Loyal was slow going. Light rain continued to fall, the temperature continued to balance on the edge of freezing, and ice continued to build up, layer upon layer, coating asphalt and trees and power lines alike.

Grace stared through the Nova's windshield, eyebrows tilted low and arms crossed over her chest. "What if the power goes out? It's supposed to get colder."

"Honey, we'll just have to deal with that if it happens."

"Can you drop me off at home so I can check on them?"

Of course, the horses.

Under normal circumstances, Val would jump at the idea. Grace had already visited the morgue and the scene of a brutal murder, even if they didn't actually enter the room. That was a lot for a sixteen year old to handle in a day. But with Hess still out there …

"I'm sorry, Grace. You need to stick with me for now."

"It's Dixon Hess, isn't it? You think he'll come after us next."

Val opened her mouth, then closed it before any lies could slip out. Protecting Grace was vital, but she couldn't give empty reassurances. Her niece seemed to have forgiven her for keeping the multiple sclerosis a secret. Following that with another fib might destroy the trust they had left. "He won't come after us if we don't give him the opportunity. That's why you need to stay where it's safe."

"Okay. If you agree to stay safe, too."

"That's a deal."

The streets of Lake Loyal were deserted, the businesses lining Elmwood closed for the weather. Grace had been right about the temperature dropping, but instead of the cold transforming rain into snow or sleet, it continued to fall as liquid and freeze on whatever surface it hit. Even salt was no longer able to keep up.

Of course, businesses being closed didn't mean the police station was. And as usual, Oneida was running the show. Spotting Val and Grace in the vestibule, she clamored to the entrance to let them in. "Chief. Am I glad to see you."

Val let herself smile inwardly at the fact that she was apparently still chief in Oneida's eyes, then got down to business. "What's going on?"

"What isn't going on? With all the car crashes and downed power lines setting off alarms and the fire over at Dale Kasdorf's place, we're scrambling to cover it all."

"Did you call Becca in?"

"Sure did. She just got here. Sergeant Olson, too. Chief Schneider called earlier to say he's having car trouble, but he promised to be in long before now."

Val had to wonder if the trouble wasn't with his usual car but with a dented front fender he sustained on a truck after running her off the road last night. "Where's Olson?"

"In the briefing room. He's bringing Becca and Jimmy Weiss up to speed."

Arranging for Grace to hang out with Oneida in dispatch, Val descended into the station's basement.

She heard the hum of Olson's voice before she saw him. Standing at the front of the tiny room, he was reviewing all the balls they had in the air for the extra officers who'd been called in … in this case, all they had. Becca and a businesslike little bulldog named Weiss.

He'd just finished warning them about the dangers of exploding ordnance in the fire at Kasdorf's place when he spotted her.

"Okay. That's it. Get out there and be safe." He crossed the room before the two officers had moved out of their chairs. "You heard about Monica?"

"I just came from the hotel."

"You shouldn't have come back. He's not going to stop. You don't think that fire at Kasdorf's is an accident."

"No."

"So who's next? You?"

"Probably. Or Lund."

"Where is he?"

"Fighting the fire."

"That's great. Just great." He shook his head. Long fingers opening and closing into fists by his side, he was more upset than she'd seen him since that day at the lake when he was standing over Kelly's body.

She was having a hard enough time controlling her own worry. She didn't need Olson adding to it. "Take it easy, Pete. He's not coming after me here at the station, and I doubt he's going to attack Lund in front of all the firefighters in the district and a few officers, too."

"So he won't get you this second. But how about an hour from now? How about later tonight?"

Val peered around Olson's shoulder. Both officers appeared absorbed in organizing their equipment, but they were obviously doing more listening than anything else.

She gave Olson a hard stare. "Why don't we go up to my office?" Even though technically it was no longer hers.

"We can't stay on top of this, let alone get ahead of him. Not with the ice." Olson continued as if he hadn't heard. "I just learned there's a pile up on the interstate. Trucks and cars backed up for miles. Emergency vehicles can't get through. State troopers are tied up dealing with that. County is talking about going in on snowmobiles. They've asked that we send anyone we can spare. But Chief, we don't have enough people as it is."

"We'll figure it out, Sergeant." She injected command into her voice, hoping he would take the hint and pull himself together and that the officers listening would feel confident someone was in control.

He nodded, as if finally catching on to her concerns. Sweat beaded along his hairline, and he brushed a hand over his shorn head, wiping it away. "I tried calling, texting, couldn't reach you."

"Schneider is acting chief."

"He hasn't been in today. That's why Oneida asked me to come in."

So everything was falling apart. She probably should feel vindicated that the Lake Loyal PD couldn't run without her, instead she just felt overwhelmed. But not as overwhelmed as Olson. A situation she might as well use to her advantage. She scooped in a deep breath. "I found out who Jane Doe is, Pete."

A muscle along his jaw flexed. He looked away, focusing on the wall.

"I have to wonder if you already know."

He glanced around the room.

Weiss was already gone and Becca was on her way out.

"Do you want to talk upstairs?"

He stepped to the door, closed it, then leaned back as if he wasn't able to take another step. "I took her to him, Val."

She frowned. "Who? Elizabeth Unger?"

He shook his head. "I never knew Liz Unger. Kelly. She was afraid. She needed help. Hess was such a bastard. And she was afraid her husband …" He looked down at the floor. "So I took her to him."

"Took her to who?"

"Chief Schneider."

"I'm not following you, Pete. He was the chief of police. If she needed help, why *wouldn't* you take her to him?"

"The chief helped her disappear."

That was the connection she needed. "He framed Hess?"

He looked back at the floor, nodding. "I didn't know. Not when we were investigating. I thought it was Lund at first, just like you. Then I was sure it was Hess."

"But when we found Kelly's body in the lake?" she prompted. She remembered how distressed Olson had been that day. Even though it had been cold, he'd been sweating, just as he was now.

"Yeah, that's when I started to wonder."

"And you didn't say anything."

"No."

"Pete, Liz Unger was married to Schneider. Still is, actually."

He swallowed, his Adam's apple sliding up and down several times, but he didn't speak.

She waited a few beats, gave him a chance to think, then she delivered the question. "Did Jeff kill Elizabeth Unger?"

"I don't know."

"I think you do."

He shook his head, finally meeting her eyes. "I never thought he killed her. That didn't even occur to me."

"But you knew he framed Hess."

"After Kelly turned up in the lake, yes."

"Where did you think the body in the barrel came from?"

"I don't know. I guess I assumed he got it from a cemetery or funeral home or something."

"Assumed? You must have discovered some things that didn't add up when you were looking into Kelly's family."

"What things?"

"That the police report on the car accident that killed her doesn't exist? That the cemetery where she's supposed to be buried knows nothing about it?"

He said nothing, just shook his head.

"Why didn't you bring these things to my attention? This time we were looking at Kelly's maternal relatives specifically. Were you helping him cover up?"

"What I did, it wasn't a cover up."

"What was it?"

"He said he was looking into it, asked me to be patient while he sorted out the answers. I trusted him. I took his word and didn't check myself."

"Sounds like you were willing to help him cover up the fact that he framed Hess."

Olson said nothing, not that there was anything he could say.

"You weren't surprised when I asked if Jeff killed his wife just now," Val said, her voice low. It was important for her to know what Pete suspected and when. It was vital that she figure out if she could trust Pete at all.

"Honestly? I would have been until yesterday."

"What happened yesterday?"

"Harlan called just as the chief was leaving for the day. He asked what insurance the PD had ten years ago, because he was trying to track down some old medical records."

"But that didn't mean Liz was murdered."

"No, but the chief's reaction told me something was wrong." He crossed the two feet to a table and leaned a hip on the edge, as if he was too exhausted to stand any longer. "I tried to call you."

She told him about the truck running her off the road.

Pete just stared, agitation gone, the stoic Norwegian she knew back in place. "The chief has an old truck. He bought it to go hunting after he retired. We can probably match the damage and paint transfer."

She nodded. She probably shouldn't be so fast to forgive Olson, but she could sense his loyalties had changed. Or maybe, with the ice Armageddon waging outside and two men wanting her dead, she couldn't be too picky about her allies.

"I think it's time we have a talk with the chief. I'd like to get out there before he has a chance to ditch the truck. And if Liz Unger really did die ten years ago, Schneider had to have been keeping her body somewhere."

"You want me to call county? See if I can get a cadaver dog?"

"I doubt they can get one out to his house until tomorrow, but yeah, give them a call, see what they say."

A knock sounded on the door.

"Come on in," Val said, bracing herself for the next bout of what almost had to be bad news.

Becca stood in the doorway. "We got a call back from the State Crime Lab. Oneida sent me to tell you."

Val's stomach gave a little hitch. Oneida wouldn't send a messenger. Not unless she didn't want Grace, who was with her in dispatch, to hear. "We've sent a lot to the lab. What is it?"

"A tissue. I collected it along with a bunch of other stuff from the shore."

And here she'd chalked that up to a long shot. She couldn't check the smile that spread over her lips. Sometimes it paid to be thorough. "Please tell me they found DNA."

"They did."

Hot Damn. "And they have a result? Already?" It had only been a week.

"I had Harlan pressure them to expedite. And I suggested he say it was tied to the inquiry into the Hess investigation."

Val had to admit, she was impressed. "Good job."

Becca beamed like a little kid showing off for her parents. "We now know who was with Kelly Lund right before she died."

Chapter
Twenty-Four

Lund would have liked to follow Val's advice and just let the old Kasdorf shack burn. But as he pulled Unit One up a good distance behind the pumper truck and surveyed the scene, he knew it wasn't going to be so easy.

He wasn't sure if Kasdorf had been rescuing his collection or if firefighters had pulled the weapons away from the flame, but one look at the stockpile of ammunition stacked on a tarp a safe distance from the fire suggested there was likely more inside.

The guy was obviously a little off.

Not that you couldn't tell just by looking at the house. Old farm houses were common as grass in the area, but this one boasted an extra layer of crazy and neglect like none he'd seen. Windows were half boarded up, half covered with opaque and yellowed sheets of plastic. Bales of molded hay wrapped the foundation, extra insulation or bulletproofing, he wasn't sure. Add that to the chipped paint and sagging roof, and the place looked like it was haunted by insane ghosts.

Pulling his eyes from the house, he scanned the rest of the situation.

Chief Fruehauf was at the scene tonight. Pushing sixty, he'd stopped attending every call as he had when Lund first joined the department, instead concentrating on making sure the paid volunteers had the training and equipment they needed to do their jobs. The boring, administrative, sometimes political tasks, things Lund didn't want to go near.

But the man knew fires as well. From a glance, Lund could tell the chief was playing it safe, setting up healthy perimeter around the fire to protect from the possible fragmentation hazard.

He climbed out of the truck and slung his SCBA over his shoulders like a back pack. In the big rigs, the rear seats held the air tanks on the back of each seat, save the driver's. As soon as a firefighter sat down, he could just slip on the gear and be good to go. Since Unit One handled everything from assisting EMS to extrication to fire, it had to be more flexible.

In this case, it meant it took him longer to get ready.

Dempsey was already there, leaning on a split rail fence that looked so rotten, it might collapse under him at any moment. Face flushed he had his face shield up and SCBA mask hanging around his neck. He clutched a sports drink in one fist, more than half the bottle of bright orange sugar water gone.

He looked up at Lund's approach. "He's in there, man. Kasdorf. The idiot."

Lund nodded toward the pile. "Let me guess. Saving his guns."

"Dumb ass is going to get himself killed. I wouldn't be surprised if he's already given in to the smoke."

"Have you been inside?"

"Found that ammo just inside the door, and got it the hell out of there. I kept thinking every snap and pop from the fire was a round going off."

Lund gave him a nod and started in the chief's direction.

"Wait," called Dempsey. "You going in?"

Lund turned back in time to see him chug the rest of his drink and lurch to his feet. "You're not ready to go back yet."

"Just needed a drink."

Lund shook his head. "You can pull me out after one of those rounds takes me down."

Dempsey shot him an exaggerated frown. "Then I'll hope the guy has something more explosive. At least then some of you will find your way out here all on your own."

The chuckle loosened the tightness in Lund's chest. He caught up with the chief.

"About time you got here," the chief said.

"Soon as I could."

"We've been holding off, just trying to contain it, keep it from spreading to the trees and outbuildings. We know he has some explosives in there and ammunition, of course."

"I want to go in, see if I can get him out."

The chief didn't even blink. "Okay. Take Sandoval."

Almost a foot shorter than Lund, Sandoval was one of the toughest guys he'd ever known. Former military and just back from Afghanistan, he could face down any situation without a blink. Lund nodded. "Perfect."

"And Kevlar."

Lund groaned inwardly at the thought of wearing body armor under his heavy turnout gear. Even if it was only a vest, he would be dripping sweat before he even got close to the fire.

But orders were orders. He peeled off his gear and put on the vest Dempsey handed him. After getting redressed, Lund hooked up his SCBA and donned his mask.

He took his first breath, stomach hitching a little bit at the split second delay, then the air started flowing and his breath settled into rhythm. He pulled the soft hood over the back of his head, attached all the straps, and put on his helmet. Dempsey checked him over, then Sandoval, fussing with covering every inch of skin as if they were little boys going out to play in the snow.

In minutes, they were ready.

Smoke billowed from the open front door, and as soon as Lund stepped through, he couldn't see a thing.

Sandoval took the lead. Left hand skimming the wall, he crawled on hands and knees, shouting out when he reached a window, door, or any other feature Lund needed to be aware of.

Also on hands and knees, Lund kept his left hand in contact with Sandoval's boot. While Sandoval guided along the walls, Lund's job was to search for Kasdorf. Stretching, he skimmed his right hand in front of him and swept his right leg toward the room's center.

Sweat ran down Lund's back in steady streams, beaded his forehead and stung his eyes. Not for the first time, he wished the department had the funds for thermal imaging cameras. The devices made seeing through smoke and darkness a breeze, picking up both the heat of flame and body heat of victims.

Without the technology, the going was much slower. Luckily Kasdorf had little furniture, so little, in fact, that Lund had to wonder if he lived in the house at all.

After finally completing their sweep, Sandoval paused. "Upstairs or down?"

Lund thought for a second. He knew little about the man, but Val had mentioned his survivalist tendencies and hatred of police. If threatened, he'd guess someone like that would burrow underground. And with all this smoke, that was probably the only place he might still be able to breathe. "Down."

On the move again, Sandoval led back through the kitchen to the cellar door. They rose to their feet and walked down the stairs, the smoke thinning from too thick to see your hand to disconcerting gloom. Like many old farmhouses, the cellar was made of stone, water seeping through the chinks between. With the SCBA, Lund couldn't smell a thing, but dank mildew was a good bet.

Movement stirred in the corner.

He squinted through mask and face shield, trying to focus through the gloom, but could make out nothing but phantoms of smoke from above.

They searched the area on their feet this time. Like the first floor, the cellar was relatively uncluttered, just an old chest freezer, a new hot water heater, furnace and water softener. And a wall of shelves lined with canning jars.

It couldn't be. The whole idea was ridiculous. And yet ...

Lund braced a hand against one side of the shelves and shoved.

Solid.

Apparently he'd guessed wrong. Kasdorf wasn't the burrowing type. The man must be on the second floor. There was no way he could have survived the smoke up there. Lund had likely failed to save his third victim in a week.

He turned to direct Sandoval up the stairs only to see the phantom materialize behind him ... but it was no phantom.

It was a man holding a big-ass handgun.

Chapter
Twenty-Five

Val couldn't wait any longer for the big reveal. "So who was with Kelly before she died?"

Becca glanced at Olson, then back to Val, but didn't answer.

A nervous shimmy started right below her rib cage. "Spit it out, Becca."

"David Lund."

Val's throat constricted.

Pete narrowed his eyes on the rookie. "So we recovered a used tissue with David Lund's DNA in it from the scene? He was there that morning. Couldn't he have blown his nose?"

Becca shook her head. "It wasn't from him blowing his nose."

"Semen?"

She nodded. "Some killers ... get excited when they take a life."

Val's mind stuttered. What Becca was saying was impossible. She couldn't wrap her mind around it.

"And if you remember," Becca continued, "we had snow the day before, so a tissue couldn't have been there long without being dissolved by the elements."

Pete focused on Val. "Are we going to bring him in?"

Val forced a nod, although her mind was screaming. It didn't feel right, but that was the problem, wasn't it? When it came to Lund, she'd been going by her feelings since Kelly's body showed up in the lake. Could she have been wrong? Could she have slept with a killer?

She felt sick and tired and numb and ready to throw in the towel on the whole thing. But she couldn't do that, could she? She had to do the job, even though it was not technically hers to do. There was no one else.

She cleared her throat, but the dry constriction remained. "We pay the chief a visit first. Then we talk to Lund."

Val hated the idea of letting Grace out of her sight, but she certainly wasn't going to drag the girl to either an arrest or what could be a rather explosive fire. Besides, when push came to shove, the safest place in Lake Loyal was sitting in the dispatch center of the police station, Oneida feeding her sugar cookies and mothering her with the ferocity of a grizzly.

For now, circumstances required officers to stop responding to crashes where no one was hurt. Her entire department was focused on helping the injured and assisting the county sheriff's department and state patrol with the interstate pileup nightmare.

That left two cars. Becca took the remaining black-and-white, and Olson and Val piled into his SUV. She left Jack's Nova safely parked.

The chief had retired to a remodeled seventies split level in a wooded development on the north side. It wasn't far, but Olson drove so slowly, Val thought they probably would've arrived sooner on foot. Each time he tapped the brakes, the vehicle slid in slow motion several yards through a stop sign or toward a ditch, before the curb or lack of momentum would bring them to a stop.

If she'd thought the trees were breathtaking this morning, tonight they were otherworldly, except in the spots where it appeared as though a tornado had blown through. Supple branches sparkled like glass and arched under heavy ice, sometimes reaching all the way to the ground. Larger and older branches snapped and hung like a scene from a disaster movie. It was a miracle anyone in the area still had power.

By the time they reached the chief's place, her back was covered with clammy sweat, and every nerve in her body was starting to feel as useless as her hand and her right eye.

Even in the early dark of a cloudy late afternoon, no lights were on in the house. They parked in the driveway, Becca pulling in behind them.

Deciding to take the straightforward approach, they climbed from their vehicles, marched up to the front door, and rang the bell.

Nothing.

Val shielded the glass side light from the glow to the west and peered through the glass.

As in most split level houses, the front door opened to a small landing. Half a flight of stairs stretched upward to the main floor, the other half led down, a difficult floor plan to manage for people with disabilities ... and for police.

At the top of the stairs, a small table rested on its side. The clock that had once set on top lay beside it, crystal shattered, pieces scattered down the stairs.

"Olson." She stepped away from the window and motioned for him to look.

His body stiffened, and he drew his gun. Becca did the same.

Val could only wish she had hers. Another casualty of her suspension. She reached for the door knob. It twisted under her hand. Pausing, she eyed the two of them.

They nodded.

She pushed the door open.

Olson then Becca flowed into the house. They climbed the stairs, guns ready, footfalls scuffing lightly on tile.

Val stayed on the landing, keeping an eye on the dark yawn of the lower level. The harder she tried to hear what was going on upstairs, the louder her pulse drummed. Seconds crawled, ticked off by the broken clock's still functioning hands.

Finally Olson appeared at the top landing, lips pinched with tension, brows low. "Upper two levels are clear. Take a look."

He descended, Becca following, and the two passed Val and continued to the lower level.

Val climbed the stairs.

The table and clock were only the beginning. The rest of the living room was a wreck as well. A lamp was shattered, a chair tipped over, papers strewn around. She could only conclude it was the scene of a brawl.

She stepped around the mess and into the kitchen. Compared to the living room, things were neat in here. But the items that were out of place gave her a chill.

A knife block had been knocked to the floor, knives scattered across the counter. The chef's knife nowhere to be found.

The dining room was all that was left on this level. She picked her way to the doorway, stepping carefully as not to disturb any evidence.

No damage here. The hardwood floor showed no scuffs, the chairs sat straight in their places, even the bills, calculator and checkbook were still spread across the table top, undisturbed.

Blowing out a breath of relief, she circled the table.

The missing knife lay on the floor, its blade dull and sticky, matching the rusty stain on the corner of the oriental rug.

The bullet went wide.

Lund went in low.

With each step, he waited for the slug to connect, braced himself for the pain.

He hit the man square in the gut, plowing into him like a linebacker, driving with his legs, just as another explosion pummeled his ears.

The man flew backward, bounced on the floor once, then slammed into the chest freezer, Lund on top of him. His weapon clattered loose and skittered across the floor.

Holding the guy's arms against his sides, Lund took a look at his face.

Buzz cut and scruffy beard, he squinted, eyes barely open. His skin was flushed pink, as if he'd spent too long in a sauna, but Lund knew his biggest problem wasn't excessive heat, but the carbon monoxide he'd been breathing while trying to save his precious weapons store.

"We've got to get this guy out," he called to Sandoval. His ears rang, head throbbed. He could hardly hear his own voice. "Give me a hand."

Sandoval didn't answer. Or maybe Lund couldn't hear.

Keeping one hand on Kasdorf's chest, he twisted around to search for his fellow firefighter. The smoke seemed to be growing thicker, even down here, and it took a few seconds before he could make out distant shapes in the dark gloom.

Sandoval was in front of the fake shelves, face down on the cellar floor.

The house cleared and no sign of Chief Schneider, save possibly the blood in the dining room, Val allowed Olson to lead her to the outbuilding in back.

If Chief Schneider had done the things she suspected, she probably shouldn't be so worried about him now. But no matter what he'd done, she'd cared about him, admired him, respected him, and she couldn't shut those feelings off like a spigot.

The meager glow of the sun had faded completely, though Val wasn't sure if it had set or the clouds were just too thick for its last rays to poke through. Walking the short distance across the yard was dangerously slick, ice skates probably more valuable now than boots.

Once a pole barn, probably designed for horses, the steel structure hadn't seen animals of any kind for years. Now home to boxes, an old refrigerator and what looked like a vehicle hidden under a tarp, the place smelled of mouse droppings and dust, and although they were sheltered from the pattering rain, the metal walls seemed to intensify the chill.

At least she couldn't detect the scent of blood.

Olson and Becca moved quickly, leading with their weapons. They cleared the building, then moved to the vehicle and pulled the tarp off a pickup truck.

"No one inside." Becca called.

Val let out a breath and crossed the cluttered dirt floor.

"No, but get a load of this." Olson pointed to the scraped up bumper and left fender. Traces of bright green marred the paint.

For a moment, Val just stared. A long ago murder she could keep distant, more of a mental puzzle than a visceral reality. The fact that Schneider had tried to kill her just last night to cover up his crime wasn't as easy to compartmentalize.

But she still didn't want to see him dead.

Becca's radio broke the moment, crackling to life, Oneida's voice booming out the call. "Shots fired. 1324 Sunrise Ridge Road. Shots fired."

Val didn't need to check the GPS to know the address belonged to one Dale W. Kasdorf.

Chapter
Twenty-Six

With no handcuffs, no rope, no nothing to secure Kasdorf, Lund didn't dare leave him to check on Sandoval. At best, the guy would probably scurry back to wherever he'd been hiding and die of carbon monoxide poisoning. At worst, he'd get his hands on another weapon and make sure he finished both Sandoval and him.

So he did the only thing he could do. He pulled back his fist and nailed the nutbag in the jaw.

A pair of night vision goggles that had flown off when he'd tackled Kasdorf proved to be broken, and Lund tossed them aside. Taking the rifle, he crossed the basement to Sandoval and knelt by his side. "Jorge?"

The firefighter was breathing, the hiss of his respirator mixing with Lund's. A groan shuddered through his body.

"Can you move, man? I've got to get you out of here."

Another groan.

Lund decided to take that as a yes.

Grasping a shoulder, he slowly rolled Sandoval to his side. Through his mask, he could see the man's eyes were open, though flinching in pain. He scanned his coat.

There was a rip in the side of his chest, but no blood. Not that he was sure he'd be able to see an injury through the thick turnout gear and darkness. "Can you stand up?"

Sandoval mumbled something, then struggled to comply.

Lund took one arm and pulled him to his feet. He shuffled him up against the shelving. "Hold on, okay? I'll be right back."

Sandoval nodded, his face a grimace.

On his way back to collect Kasdorf, Lund pulled out his radio, but try as he might, all he got was static. Damn paranoid bastard was probably jamming the signal. He slung the man across his shoulders in a fireman's carry and returned to Sandoval.

They were on their own.

"Lean on me."

"I can make it. Go on, get him out."

He could barely hear the words, ears still ringing, but it wasn't tough to figure out the message. "Do you always have to be a pain in the ass? Lean on me, anyway."

Sandoval chuckled a touch, then doubled over in pain.

The going was slow, each step an ordeal. They crossed the basement easily enough, but the stairs proved to be immeasurably difficult. More than once Lund thought about leaving Sandoval, taking Kasdorf out, then coming back. But then what? If the place collapsed, he would have sacrificed a good man for the nut who shot him, and he just couldn't live with that.

Sweat stung his eyes, making it tough to see. The temperature had to be seven or eight hundred degrees easy. His shirt and jeans were soaked under the heavily insulated turnout gear, but without it, he'd be cooked like Christmas turkey.

Smoke choked the main floor, and he made for the door as fast as he could. At least he and Sandoval still had their SCBA intact. Kasdorf was taking it all in, provided he was still breathing at all.

When they emerged, the first face he latched onto was Val's. She stood next to Chief Fruehauf, the rookie cop and Sergeant Olson with her.

And absolutely no sign of Dixon Hess.

Luck was smiling on both of them tonight.

Dempsey met them as soon as he stepped off the porch. "Sandoval, you hurt?"

"He was shot by Mr. Second Amendment here," Lund said.

Dempsey looped Sandoval's arm over his shoulder and half carried him away from the burning house.

The EMTs met them at the perimeter with a stretcher. Lund let them take Kasdorf, and they immediately slapped an oxygen mask on him and made for the ambulance.

Dempsey helped Sandoval take off his SCBA and coat. He studied the hole in the coat and corresponding tear in the side of the vest. "It doesn't look like it went through. Guess it was a good idea to wear these vests after all, eh Lund?"

Lund gave him a nod, although he still couldn't hear him very well over the clanging in his ears.

Dempsey helped the injured firefighter peel off his vest. "No blood."

The round had glanced off, ripping his coat, tearing the fabric of the vest, and probably breaking a few ribs in the process, but Sandoval was going to be okay.

"You weren't even shot, you whiner." Lund gave him a smile.

Sandoval grinned back. "Yeah, I'm a real pussy. And you fell for it, helping me out of that house."

Finally able to breathe, Lund took off his own coat, despite the icy rain, and let cool wash over him. Dempsey guided Sandoval to the ambulance, and it pulled out, taking the injured firefighter and Kasdorf to the hospital. Sergeant Olson followed in the police SUV.

Val walked back toward him, the rookie officer, Schoenborn, in her wake.

While he didn't want to show it, he drank in the look of worried relief in Val's eyes. He wasn't sure if she was as taken with him as he was with her, but there seemed to be something there, something that could grow into more. At least he'd like to think so.

"David?"

He didn't remember her ever calling him by his first name, and it sounded awkward. Unnatural. "Is everything okay?"

She stopped when she reached the squad car. "Can you come over here?"

He headed down the gravel to the black and white parked on the road's shoulder.

She gave him an attempt at a smile. "I need you to come with us. There are a few things we have to talk about."

"About Kasdorf? Bastard took two shots at us."

"Yes, Kasdorf." She hesitated, as if uncomfortable continuing.

"Something else?"

"A few questions."

"Questions?" Unnatural turned to downright wrong. "What's going on?"

"We've gotten some new information."

"About what?"

"Kelly. We've discovered evidence that suggests she was with someone shortly before she died."

"That's great."

Val didn't look like she thought it was great. In fact, she looked like it was the worst thing that had happened in a while.

And he knew what her week had been like.

"Who was she with?"

"We can talk about it at the station."

"As in you have something you need my help with? Or as in you can interrogate me more effectively there?"

She stared at him, her eyes focused on his, her mouth neither frowning nor smiling but exactly neutral.

Oh, shit.

"You can't be serious."

"Please, sir." The rookie cop opened the squad car's door—the back door—and gestured for him to climb inside. "We'd like to do this with your cooperation."

He glanced back at Val.

"Please, David."

And right that moment, he knew he'd never want to hear a woman call him by his first name again.

Val had never hated her job as much as she did right that moment.

The look of betrayal on Lund's face was burned in her memory like a brand of fire. After all the suspicions she'd subjected him to the first time they'd thought Kelly died, after the truce they'd struck, after the feelings that were starting to take root between them, for her to do this was unforgivable.

Especially since deep in her heart she still couldn't believe he'd killed his wife.

So why was she doing it? Because of a DNA test? Because Becca was looking on? Because it was her job?

Damn her job.

She pulled in a shaky breath and resisted her need to turn around and check on him through the steel grating separating the front seat from the back. Seeing him in the cage, helpless, would only be piling on the humiliation. At least, she didn't have to stoop to that.

The roads were the same as when they'd driven down, skating-rink slick, but Becca was rock solid behind the wheel. Broken trees lined the road into town, branches having snapped under layers of ice. At least the radio had been quiet for the last few minutes. Not that there were any spare officers to send if a problem did arise.

Val couldn't remember ever having been stretched this thin. Not before she'd become chief and certainly not after. She just prayed Lake Loyal made it through the night.

The power seemed to still be on when they turned onto Elmwood Avenue. Ice covered pavement reflected the handful of streetlights with mirror-like clarity.

Blue-tinged piles of road salt scattered the surface but couldn't keep up with the steady patter of freezing rain. Theirs was the only car out and about, most residents smart enough to stay off the roads.

Becca pulled into the police station driveway and stopped in front of the entrance used to bring arrestees into the holding cell.

Val didn't like the idea of marching Lund in like a criminal, even in light of reality, but at this time of night, they didn't use the front entrance, so she let it slide.

She got out and opened the door for Lund, avoiding his eyes. For the first time since she got the position, she wasn't sure she wanted to be chief. Technically she was still on suspension, but with Schneider gone, no one seemed to mind too much that she was back on the job.

She led him over the slick sidewalk to the station door, hit the buzzer, and looked up into the camera. After ten at night, Oneida had to buzz people in, even officers, for security reasons. It took a few seconds for the lock to click open, and Val pushed the door wide.

"Becca, can you throw some salt down? I'm not sure it does much with the temperatures dropping, but we have to try."

"Sure thing, Chief." Becca propped the door open with a shim, grabbed the bucket of salt they kept by the door, and headed back into the night.

Val led Lund into the station, past the holding cell and to the interrogation room. Not her preference, but since her office didn't have a camera to record the interview, it would have to do. "Why don't you take a seat? I'll be right back."

He stepped up to the doorway and stopped. "You can't believe I killed her, Val."

The smell of smoke clung to him, overpowering. He was still wearing his heavy boots and the turnout overalls. The neon yellow reflecting bands encircling his legs glowed in the overhead lights. Dark hair clung to his forehead, and a smudge of soot marked one cheek.

The man had just saved two lives, and now she was supposed to prove he'd taken one? How did that make sense? "It doesn't matter what I believe."

"It does to me."

She let out a shuddering breath. "We'll talk. Be honest with me, and I'll try to make this easier."

He shook his head. "Easier? How can anything be easy when I know you don't believe me?"

She wanted to tell him she did, but that was ridiculous. She hadn't asked him about the evidence. She hadn't given him a chance to respond. A chance to explain. "Have a seat. Please. I have to check with Oneida. I'll be right back."

She strode to the door leading into the rest of the station and hit the button signaling Oneida to buzz her in. The monitors above the door showed the interrogation room where Lund was now sitting, tapping his fingers on the small table and jiggling one leg. Antsy. Caged.

Helpless.

She felt sick to her stomach.

Finally the door unlocked, and she pulled it open.

The station always felt quiet at night, but tonight Val couldn't help an accompanying ache of loneliness. She passed the darkened door to the break room and headed straight for dispatch. She couldn't wait to see Grace again, to know the one most important to her was all right, to hear all the awesome things Oneida had taught her about the inside workings of the Lake Loyal PD.

The first thing she saw as she rounded the corner was the pool of red on the floor.

Her breath hitched. She reached for her gun, racing forward, and hit nothing but her jean-clad hip.

Oneida lay face down, a plate of her famous sugar cookies scattered around her head. Reindeer, snowmen and Santa Claus soaked with blood.

"God, Oneida." Val fell to her knees. Hands shaking, she checked for a pulse. It was faint, but there. She had to call for help.

Her next thought was of Grace.

"You care about her." His voice was soft, like a distant breeze toying with wind chimes.

Val spun around.

He stood in the darkened break room entrance, Grace in front of him, hands cuffed, his arm pinning her back against his chest. He held a knife to her throat, the blade already dull with blood.

"If I'd known how you feel about the fat one, I would have made her death more painful and last much longer. Just like I plan to do with our darling Grace."

Chapter
Twenty-Seven

A hum pulsed in Val's ears, so loud she couldn't think.

Oneida wasn't dead. Not yet.

But Grace.

Her beautiful Grace in the arms of Dixon Hess.

She stared at Val, eyes red, lower lip trembling. Tears streamed down her cheeks and silent sobs wracked her body.

A wound opened inside Val, so painful she couldn't think. Grace was the only thing that mattered. Not the job, not her duty, only her precious niece.

And she was going to die.

"Let her go, Hess." Her voice sounded stronger than she felt, steady and in command. She had to pretend Oneida was dead. She had to convince him to let go of Grace. "I know you're angry. But you don't care about her. Take it out on me."

"Oh, Valerie. I'm so disappointed. Don't you remember the chat we had?"

Of course, she did. But she couldn't let herself think. Couldn't let herself put the pieces together. How Tamara the lawyer loved to talk. How Monica loved Derrick. How Kasdorf loved his guns. How Lund loved freedom and hated being helpless.

No.

Lund and Becca were still free. They still had a shot. Becca was even armed with a gun and a radio.

Val struggled to stand, her legs unsteady. If she could get to the keyboard, she could unlock the door to the holding cell. She could let Becca in. If she turned her head, she could see the security cameras' images, even with her bad eye. She would have to stall until Lund and Becca knew what was going on and could get into place to make their move.

"Do you?"

Her mind stuttered, trying to catch up with whatever he'd been saying that she hadn't heard. "I'm sorry."

He gave her a look that made her wonder if he'd already figured out her plan. "Our chat about justice. Do you remember?"

"Yes."

"What was it?"

"You felt the system wronged you. That your conviction took away everything you loved."

"Not the system and the conviction, Val. You. You wronged me. You took away everything I loved most. The rest of them wouldn't have been able to touch me if it weren't for you. And now I'm going to take away what you love."

He caressed Grace's face with the blade, tracing down her cheekbone and up under her chin. Smudges of Oneida's blood trailed behind, dark against Grace's pale skin.

Grace let out a whimper so soft it sounded like the mew of a kitten.

"Don't, Hess … Dixon … Please."

"Keep it up. I like to hear you beg. It lets me know you're listening."

"I'm listening. I was listening all along."

"No. If you had been, I never would have spent a moment in prison."

She held up her hands, palms out. "You're right. But I've tried to make it up to you. I know who the woman in the burning barrel was. I know who killed her. Let Grace leave, and I'll tell you everything."

"Let Grace leave, huh? That's all I have to do?"

"Please."

Hardness descended over his features. "I know who was in that barrel, Valerie. And I know who killed her. You have nothing to bargain with. And soon I'll make sure you have nothing at all."

She could feel her hope draining away like the strength from her hand and the sight from her eye. The screen showing the area outside the holding cell was still vacant. If Becca had come back into the building after salting the walkway, she must have done it while Hess was threatening Grace.

Her only hope was to turn on the intercom so at least Lund could hear.

She let her hands fall, but instead of bringing them to her sides, she let them rest on the table that held Oneida's computers, the intercom panel still inches away. A pewter badger paperweight she'd given her dispatcher for her last birthday sat inches from her hand.

"You never asked how I know who framed me."

He was setting some sort of trap. She could hear it in the tone of his voice, the lilting sneer of each word. She tried to see the table using her peripheral vision.

"Don't you care?"

"Of course, I care."

"Then ask."

It was a stupid game, one designed only to prove to himself that she could be controlled. But she had little choice but to play. "How do you know who framed you?"

"I know, because I looked him in the eye, and he confessed everything."

"You killed him." She'd feared it from the moment she'd seen the upended table, broken clock and blood. The thing that surprised her was the hollow feeling in her stomach, even after all Schneider had done.

"Not yet. He has yet to lose what he loves most."

"Where is he?"

Hess turned his head to glance toward the front entrance.

Val grabbed the paperweight and placed it on the intercom switch, then followed the trajectory of his gaze. "In my office?"

"Funny. He calls it his office." Hess smiled. "Go ahead. Say hello."

She didn't want to witness what he'd done to Jeff Schneider, how he would take away what Jeff loved most. Especially when she couldn't do anything to help him.

"Go." He tightened his grip on Grace, and another whimper escaped her lips.

"Okay. I'm going." She forced her feet to move, trying to brace herself for what she would see. Her senses were already overwhelmed by the odor of blood, yet somehow she detected more even before she turned the corner.

"Make it quick. You're prolonging his suffering."

She crossed the last few feet to the office and peered around the doorjamb.

Schneider was standing in the corner, totally naked.

No, not standing. Hanging.

He met her eyes, his wide and desperate. A gurgling noise came from his throat. The words criminal and liar had been carved in his chest and belly, and blood wept from the wounds.

"Chief Schneider is being punished for his crimes." Hess said from his spot in the break room. "He's been sentenced to hang by his neck until he's dead, like a common criminal. Fitting for someone who killed his wife, passed her off as Kelly Lund, and framed me. Don't you think?"

Val averted her eyes, unable to see his agony, no matter how true Hess's accusations were.

"He used you, Valerie. Set you up to take this fall. I want you to remember that when it's your time to lose what you love. I want you to remember it was your Chief Schneider who caused your pain."

Nausea made her head feel light.

"Sorry." Jeff's voice, not much more than a croak.

She opened her eyes and focused on him. The mentor she trusted. The man who had done everything Hess said. The man who would cost her Grace. And she hated him.

But she didn't want this. "This isn't justice."

"Maybe not. He should have a public trial, like I did. Have to sit there and listen to people say horrible things about him, which in his case would at least be true. He should go to prison and pray every day no one finds out he's a cop. That would take away what he loves most, force him to deny he's chief of police every day. But I don't have time for that. And this might come as a shock to you, but because of what he did, I don't trust the system. So in a roundabout way, he has himself to thank."

"You can't do this."

"Of course I can. Now would you like to hear what he told me? Would you like to hear all the horrible things he confessed to? You're not as good as a court of law crawling with TV cameras, but you're as good as I can get."

Val shook her head.

"Say yes, Valerie. Remember, I have a knife to your niece's throat."

Grace whimpered, and Val whirled around. "Yes. Yes. Go ahead."

"It seems his wife had an accident many years ago. She ran into something … oh yeah, her husband's fist. And even though he meant to keep her around to beat up on another day, she hit her head on the kitchen counter. Dead. So sad."

Val glanced back at Schneider, but he wouldn't meet her eye.

"And then what did our follow-the-law police chief do? He stuffed her in a freezer and pretended she ran away with another guy."

Val could take the story from there. She could tell Hess that after a few years, when most of Liz's family was dead, Schneider had sneaked a death certificate into a pile of papers he needed Harlan Runk to sign. With a stroke of Harlan's pen, Elizabeth Unger had died in a car wreck. And since the Unger family owned a plot in a cemetery, complete with stone waiting to be filled out, all Schneider had to do was wait until anyone who cared was dead and pretend Liz Unger had been put to rest.

"So after a bunch of years go by and wifey is all shriveled up and freezer burned, Kelly asks the police chief for help, and he sees his opportunity not only to take her and my baby away from me but to clear out his freezer for hunting season. So he torches her in the barrel and calls Valerie Ryker in to figure it all out. Isn't that right, Chief Schneider?"

Schneider swayed on his feet. He looked horrible, weak, like he couldn't last much longer.

Val had to do something. She turned back to Hess. "So why kill him? Why not let him live with the world knowing what he did, who he really is?"

"You make a compelling argument. But I think you're too late. He's already decided he's too chicken shit to face real justice."

She spun back around in time to see Schneider stagger and sag forward, as if he didn't have the strength to stand one more second. Or maybe he didn't have the will.

No.

Val raced into the office. Grabbing him around the chest in a bear hug, she tried to hold him upright. The blood from his wounds made his skin slick.

"Let him go, Valerie."

The smell of urine and blood made her head swim. Her right hand wouldn't hold, the fingers worthless. He was heavy, so heavy.

"I'll give you a choice. Step away or I start carving up the little girl."

She gasped for breath. He would kill Grace anyway. She knew that. As soon as Schneider was dead, Hess would focus on punishing Val by torturing Grace. Killing her in front of Val's eyes.

Grace's whimper crescendoed.

Val let go.

"Step away."

God help her, she did.

Where in the hell was that cop?

When Lund had first heard Hess's voice drifting through the intercom system, he'd thought it had to be a recording, a joke, something.

It didn't take long to figure out it was real.

He tried the door out of the interrogation room again, even though he knew it wouldn't budge. Damn, damn, damn. He was trapped. Utterly helpless. And just feet away Hess was going to kill Val, he was going to kill Grace. And Lund could do nothing but listen to them die.

How long could it take to salt a sidewalk?

"Oh, don't be upset about him." The voice again, over the intercom. *"He had it coming. You know he did."*

He heard a soft mewing, probably Grace.

That poor, poor girl.

He jerked the door latch again and again, but nothing he did mattered.

"Check him," Hess ordered.

Time ticked by, finally Lund picked up Val's faint voice. *"He's dead."*

"Too bad. Look at him, hanging there. Pitiful." Hess sounded happy, almost giddy. *"He was the one who started this. Kelly never would have left if it wasn't for him. She was mine."*

Lund's throat tightened. Years ago, he'd come to terms with the fact that Kelly didn't love him. He'd been her savior, and he'd told himself that was good enough for him. But he didn't believe for one second that she belonged to Hess.

He never would.

"He took her away from me."

"You didn't love Kelly." Val's voice sounded strong. Unbowed.

"I didn't say I loved her. I said she was mine. The baby was mine. Schneider and you and the lawyers, none of you had the right to take them from me."

Lund's mind stuttered. He couldn't have heard right. What baby?

A metallic clink sounded. At first Lund thought it was the cop walking back into the building. Then he realized it came over the speaker.

"Put them on. Hands in front."

Handcuffs.

"Do it."

"I ... can't. I have a problem with my hand."

"Do it or Grace gets cut."

"*Please. I'll let you put them on, but I can't fasten the other side myself.*"

The braced open outer door rattled.

Lund sprang for it, pulling it open. "It's Hess—"

Words jamming in his throat, he stared into the barrel of a gun for the second time that day.

"Back off. Hands up," the rookie said.

Oh, hell. He did as she ordered. "Hess is in the station. He has Val and her niece, and Schneider and Oneida, too. I think Schneider is dead."

"Turn around. Hands against the wall."

"You have to call for help. You have to stop him." He didn't want to have to take the gun from her, but he would try. Even if it likely meant getting shot in the process. "Listen. The intercom is on. You can hear him."

She paused.

Silence from the speaker.

"Against the wall."

"You can't think I'm making this up."

"Do it. If what you say is true, I'll release you."

He blew a breath through tight lips. "All right." He assumed the position. She clapped the handcuffs on one wrist then the other.

"Now go call for back up."

"Not until I know you're telling the truth. Come on."

She marched him out into the hall.

He waited to hear Hess's voice, to prove to the rookie that what he said was true.

She stepped up to the door leading into the station just as Hess's voice reached them. "*What do you say I start by carving my initials in her cheek?*"

Lund twisted around, trying to meet Schoenborn's eyes. "Is that enough proof for you?"

Too late.

She'd already hit the button signaling someone in the dispatch center to buzz her in.

Val was still struggling to close the handcuff around her left wrist when the buzzer sounded.

She froze. Her heart beat hard enough to break a rib. The reality of the situation cut into her like the cold edge of Hess's blade.

Any surprise entrance Becca and Lund might have made was gone. All the killer had to do was look into the dispatch center monitors and he'd know they weren't alone.

She could only pray Becca had called for help. That a tactical team was waiting to charge in, somehow out of sight. But even as she concocted the scenario in her mind, she knew it was impossible.

Gripping Grace by the hair, Hess dragged her into the dispatch center and looked up at the monitors, then down at the paperweight depressing the intercom's talk button. "Think you're smart, huh?"

Then before Val could make sense of it, he hit the button and the door buzzed open.

Lund stepped through first, his hands behind his back.

Becca followed, pushing Lund in front of her with one hand, she held her gun in the other.

Val opened her mouth to warn them about Hess, but stopped before uttering a sound.

Because Becca didn't need a warning. She had to have heard Hess's voice over the intercom. She had to know he was here.

Becca shoved Lund a few steps in front of her gun, then turned a smile on Hess. "Hi, Daddy. I'm home."

Chapter
Twenty-Eight

"Daddy?" Val echoed. She glanced from Becca to Dixon Hess and felt something inside her snap.

All along the question had been not who wanted Kelly dead, but who wanted her found. And the only answer was Dixon Hess.

And the daughter nobody knew about.

The rookie had been the one to discover Kelly's body, not Lund. She'd found her while on routine patrol. She'd also been the one to pick up garbage from the shore, including the tissue with Lund's DNA.

Val hadn't noticed before, but every bit of evidence pointing to Lund as Kelly's murderer had come from Becca. She'd had her hand in it all. It was as clear to her as a signed confession. "You killed Kelly. Didn't you, Becca? You found her. And somehow forced her to walk out on that ice."

"I had to. He was innocent." She stared at Val, looking the same as she always did, young, pretty, a good cop in the making.

How could this be happening?

"Put him over there." One hand gripping Grace's hair and the other holding the knife, Hess nodded to a chair one of the sergeants had left in the doorway of his cubicle. "And throw some leg shackles on him."

Becca marched Lund dutifully to the cubicle wall, shoved him into the chair and brought out the chains.

All the instances when Hess knew things he shouldn't have ricocheted through Val's mind. Tamara Wade's well-timed habeas corpus motion. Grace's schedule at school. The hotel where Monica and Derrick were staying.

Becca knew or could have easily learned all of those things, then conveyed them to Hess.

There was only one thing she couldn't account for. "How did you let him know about Schneider? Since you found out, you've been with me."

Becca peered up from her task and shot her a look of disdain a high school mean girl would envy. "You think I didn't know until tonight? You were the one who sent me to Harlan."

Harlan. She should have figured that. Harlan would tell an attractive woman like Becca everything she wanted to know. And a few more things she didn't.

"You really were indispensable, Valerie." Hess chuckled. "Guess you were telling the truth. You do believe in justice."

Val leaned back against the wall outside her office door and tried to stay upright.

Grace.

Lund.

If not for her, neither one would be here. If not for her, Hess never would have hurt Oneida. He never would have learned Jeff Schneider set him up.

It really was all her fault.

The overhead lights flickered. Once. Twice. Ice weighing down the power lines outside.

"So now you're going to kill us?" Lund asked.

"Not all. Not right away." Hess pulled Grace's hair, forcing her head back, her body tight against his chest.

A low sound came from her throat, a shuddering moan, as if she was too afraid to form words. Blood trailed down her cheek and neck.

Her beautiful niece. Her brilliant niece. The girl whose greatest joy was helping someone else.

"Grace is going to die first."

"No." Val lurched forward before she was aware she was moving.

Hess brought the blade to her niece's throat. "Stop."

Somehow Val found the strength to halt.

"Back up. Against the wall. Or it's over right now."

Her breath rasped in her ears, mixing with the mewing again coming from Grace.

Stupid, stupid, stupid.

What was she thinking rushing him like that? Hess wasn't a man she could intimidate with a rush of action. She needed to stall, buy time. She needed to keep him talking, find a way out of this.

She returned to the wall and eyed the front door.

She was close, only a few feet. Not that she would ever run out and leave them in the first place, and she supposed Hess knew that. But as bad as the weather was, no emergency calls had come in since she arrived. Without car wrecks to keep them busy, officers would eventually return to the station, especially those called in to deal with the ice storm.

"You're thinking someone is going to come back and save you, aren't you Valerie?"

Bringing her focus back to Hess, she kept quiet. She'd telegraphed her thoughts by looking at the door, and she wasn't about to open her mouth and give him more insight.

"No one's coming."

"They're all very busy," Becca said. "It only sounds quiet because the county has taken over dispatch. We have a weather emergency out there. The interstate has gotten worse. It's totally blocked."

She sounded happy, like a little kid talking about a snow day.

Val wanted to jam those shackles down her throat.

"What I was saying was that Grace dies first. Don't worry, Valerie, I'll make it painful and slow." He traced the blade up Grace's neck and over her lips, then nodded toward Lund. "And fireman here will sit and watch, unable to do anything to stop me. Helpless. Worthless. Impotent."

Lund sat expressionless except for a muscle working along his jaw.

Becca yanked the chain tight around his boots and turnout pants, then trussed his legs together.

"And Valerie?" Hess said.

She turned her attention back to him.

"Do you know what you'll be doing?"

ANN VOSS PETERSON

"Planning how I'm going to take that knife and gut you?"

He smiled, showing teeth so straight and white that even with her vision problems she had little trouble seeing them. "Maybe, maybe. But you're also going to stand there and know that this never would have happened to our little Grace if it weren't for you."

He pressed the blade into the skin of her cheek.

Grace screamed and struggled to jolt away, but his grip prevented it.

A sob stuck in Val's throat. The pair of cuffs still dangling around her left wrist rattled and hit the wall, but she didn't move. Not this time.

"That's better."

"Then what will you do next?" Lund's voice sounded even, strong.

Val forced herself to breathe, to think. Yes. Keep him talking. Look for an out. Lund was obviously thinking along the same lines she was, at least as she had been before fear for Grace had wiped her mind utterly clean.

"After our pretty little Grace is dead, then it's your turn, hero."

"Lund never did anything to you," Val said, somehow finding a remnant of strength in her voice. "The only thing he testified to was your affair with Kelly."

"True. And I've caused him a good deal of pain. But his death is really about you, Valerie. All this has really been about you. And from what Rebecca has told me, you have a little crush on the firefighter here. So you get to see him die, too."

254

His words didn't shock her anymore. Nor did the depth of Becca's betrayal. Now she could feel all of it gather into a toxic ball and harden in the pit of her stomach.

"And then you kill me," she said.

"You don't get off that easy."

"You don't kill her?" Becca's voice squeaked. Finished with Lund, she straightened and rested her hand on her holster.

"He wants me to live on, to know what I've lost, to know he's taken everything I loved."

"You *were* listening."

"I was."

"Then let's get started, shall we?"

Val lurched away from the wall. She needed something more to stall him. Anything. But her mind was nothing but a scream.

She would do anything to save Grace. Anything. She would willingly lay down her life, not even hesitate.

That was it.

She turned her head to look at Becca.

That was how Becca killed Kelly. How she convinced her to walk out on thin ice. "You threatened her baby."

"For God's sake, what baby?" Lund said.

She should have told him. Fuck her job, her duty, her case, and her damn insecurities. She should have told him everything and let the rest fall as it may. "Kelly's baby."

"My baby," Hess said. *"My son."*

She turned to Hess, talking to him now. "Did you ever ask her how she convinced Kelly to go with her? How she forced her to step out onto the ice?"

He lowered the knife from Grace's throat and stared at Becca. "Where is he?"

She shook her head. Glancing from Val to Hess, she took a step backward. "I don't know. I never knew."

"Then why did she willingly go with you?" Val asked.

"I had a gun on her. I was going to kill her if she didn't. Drowning or shooting, it didn't matter how she died, just that she did. Just that someone found her."

Val didn't believe her. It mattered. A lot. Becca had gone to great lengths to stage Kelly's drowning death, to make it public, to make sure she was found, to make sure Lund took the fall.

"The DNA test. You took that tissue from Lund's house, didn't you? You broke in when he was at the fire station."

"So?"

"No, shooting her wouldn't fit. You made sure Lund would be the one who pulled her out of the water, that his DNA would be discovered on that tissue, that I would arrest him for murder. The ice storm made all of this work out differently, but that was the original justice he was supposed to face."

It was half a guess, but it must have been a good one, because Becca said nothing.

Val turned on Hess. "What would make Kelly walk out on the ice? She's lived in Lake Loyal all her life. She knew it wouldn't hold her weight. She knew if she stepped out there, she was marching to her death. Why would she be willing to die without fighting back?"

"Where is he?" he repeated, louder this time.

The tension he'd been keeping on Grace's hair slackened, all his focus now drilling into his daughter.

"I was the one who got you out." Becca's voice was soft, pleading.

The lights flickered again, then went out. A second passed before the generator kicked in, bringing back the emergency lights and instruments in dispatch.

Becca took a step toward her father. "I killed her for you. I did everything for you."

Behind the rookie cop, Val noticed Lund moving his hands behind his back.

She returned her focus to Hess, but neither he nor Becca seemed aware of Lund at all, every ounce of their energy focused on the other.

"What did you do with my son?" Hess took a step forward, dragging Grace along.

She tripped on Oneida, bobbled and fell to her knees.

Val was off the wall, moving forward when Hess released her hair, letting her tumble on top of the injured dispatcher.

He raised the knife and stared at Val. "Don't move."

She took two steps back and raised her hands, palms out. She couldn't let him focus on Grace or pay too close attention to Oneida. "Ask her if the baby's still alive."

He looked back to Becca, again focused on what he wanted, what was his, what his own daughter had kept from him.

"I'm the one who loves you," she said, her voice high-pitched like a little girl's. "I would do anything for you. I have done everything. Where the baby is doesn't matter."

"My son is *all* that matters."

"I matter."

"What did you do with him?"

Becca rolled her lips toward her teeth. Even in the dim light, Val could see the sheen of tears in her eyes.

Val risked a glance in Lund's direction. Smoke curled from behind his chair, just a wisp.

The lighter he'd had in her office, the one he'd used to demonstrate flame and smolder. He was setting fire to one of the old, fabric cubicle walls.

Even with the power out, the alarms would go off. Help would come.

"She killed him," Val blurted out." She killed your baby."

Hess stared at her, those cold eyes burning. He started toward Becca. "You killed him?"

"I did not."

"After we noticed Kelly's caesarean scar, I had divers search the lake. We found his body."

"You didn't!"

Val didn't want to think too hard about what she was doing. She needed to distract Hess, she needed to give Lund a chance. "You're a rookie, Becca, and a part-timer. There are a lot of things that go on around here that you don't know."

"You took my son? You?" Hess stepped toward her.

Becca raised her weapon, first pointing at Val then at Hess. Her hands shook, tears now streaming down her cheeks.

Smoke built and spilled into the room. Becca had to have smelled it. From where he was standing, Hess could see it.

The alarm shattered the air. Water showered down from ceiling sprinklers.

Val dashed for Grace.

She could see Lund move, Becca move, and Hess too, but the water spray, the smoke, and the fact that her eyesight wasn't good in the first place, made it impossible to see much more.

She slid inside the dispatch center, reached Grace and Oneida, grabbed her niece's arm, and struggled to get her on her feet.

Behind her, Becca's gun went off.

Chapter
Twenty-Nine

Heat surged from behind Lund, smoke roiling over him, blotting out the light. He stood from the chair, took a hop forward, and fell face first to the floor.

Wriggling his body, he dragged himself forward. Becca had tightened the chains over his boots. If he could just manage to get his turnout overalls off, he could shuck the whole damn thing, boots and all.

A trick, seeing his hands were cuffed behind his back.

A scream erupted over his head. The rookie cop, he thought. Or Grace. Or Val. He couldn't tell over the blaring alarm.

Heat licked at his boots, his legs. He wasn't on fire, he knew that, just too close to it. It was a hot fire, those old separating walls burning with the ferocity he expected. Eventually the water would put it out, but he had to get far enough away that he didn't get cooked before that happened.

The smoke was a bigger problem.

He'd seen Val make a dash for it. But now he could no longer spot her. As long as she got out, saved Grace, this would work out all right.

The crack of gunfire stabbed the air.

Val?

Grace?

He pulled forward rolling his chest side to side, trying to push with his legs, but they wouldn't move. They wouldn't work.

Something was wrong.

It took a few more seconds to realize why.

He'd been shot.

Val's niece clung to her like a scared kitten. Her body trembled, breath coming hard and fast, and although Val couldn't hear anything over the fire alarm's din, she could feel sobs wracking Grace's body.

She brought her lips close to the teen's ear. "Come on, Gracie. We have to get up. You have to get up."

Smoke blotted out the emergency lights in most of the station now. Water splattered her face, her hair, and soaked into her coat. The sprinkler system should put the fire out. Maybe it already had, but it seemed like the smoke just kept coming.

"Come on, Baby. Walk with me. I need you to be strong Grace. I need your help getting Oneida out of here. She's still alive, but I can't move her without you."

The girl nodded, her hair moving against Val's cheek.

Val checked the dispatcher's pulse to make sure she was still with them. The beat was steady and sure.

She looped one of Oneida's arms around her neck and shoulder and Grace took the other.

"Good girl. Now out the front door." She wasn't sure Grace heard her, probably not. But she responded by moving forward, carrying her part of Oneida's weight.

The exit wasn't far, just around the corner. Val knew the station well. She didn't have to see.

Good thing.

The going was slow, but they got around the corner.

The alarm was even louder here, making her head throb, ears hurt. She located the door handle and placed Grace's hand on it, hoping the girl would feel the vibration of the lock release and figure out what she was asking her to do.

Feeling her way with her left hand, she found the lock release beside the door and hit the button.

She couldn't hear the door buzz, but she felt Grace pull it wide.

"Good girl."

She held her breath, half expecting Hess to grab them from behind. The three of them sidled into the vestibule, Val taking up the rear. She dipped her hand in her pockets. Finding her gloves, she stuck one in the door lock, bracing it open. She used the same trick on the outer door.

They laid Oneida under the building's overhang.

Now came the hard part.

"I have to go back for Lund. He saved us. I can't leave him in there to die." Her throat felt thick, burning, clogged by more than smoke. She shivered in the sudden cold.

Ears still ringing from the alarm, Val couldn't hear Grace's whimper, but she felt it in the grasp of her hands, the shudder wracking her shoulders.

Of course Grace wouldn't leave her. Not as easily as that. "You have to do this for me, sweetie. I need you to do this. If Oneida doesn't get help, she's not going to make it."

Grace said nothing, just clutched Val's arm hard enough to leave bruises.

"Run to the tavern. Tell them to call an ambulance and the sheriff's department. Understand?" She raised her hand to her niece's cheek.

Warm tears mixed with the sprinkler's cold spray, the girl's beautiful face knotted in distress.

"If you don't tell someone, no one will know, Grace. No one will come. Oneida will die. And the only ones who have weapons are Becca and Hess."

Finally, her head bobbed in a nod, but the tears didn't stop flowing. "I love you."

Val cupped a hand around the back of her niece's neck and gave her a quick kiss on the forehead. Her chest ached, her voice refusing to function. Releasing her, she gave her a coaxing push.

Grace gave Oneida one last look, then started in the direction of the tavern, half running, half skating.

Blinking away tears, Val scooped in a breath of fresh air, then turned and plunged back into the smoke. This time she went to her knees as soon as she'd cleared the inner door. The carpet squished under her, soaked now from the sprinklers. She couldn't see a thing in the darkness and smoke. Her eyes burned so badly, she wanted to close them.

The alarm's blare throbbed in her head. No use in listening for sound around her. She couldn't hear a thing, not even the breath in her own throat or the pounding beat of her heart. She could smell nothing but smoke, taste only ash.

Touch was her only sense.

Shuffling forward, she skimmed her hands over drenched carpet on her right, on her left. She approached the spot were Lund had been tied. The fire was out, but the smoke was still too thick to see, and all she could make out was a hazy darkness looming ahead. The hulking shape of charred cubicle walls.

From the time she'd come to Lake Loyal, the sergeants all jokingly referred to the tiny office spaces as stanchions, as if they were all cows waiting to be milked. She wasn't sure why that thought popped into her mind, but for a second she rolled it over in her thoughts the way one eats comfort food or listens to a favorite song. Those days before she'd met Dixon Hess, before she'd become chief, when everything wasn't dependent on a body that was falling apart and a mind that made too many mistakes.

She moved slowly, not wanting to miss a square inch of carpet. Her hand hit something warm. Sticky.

Leaning her weight back on her haunches, she groped heavy fabric, then flesh, still warm. She could feel the tendons in the neck, the jaw. Wisps of long hair brushed her hand. Under her fingertips, the carotid artery was deathly still.

Val's head spun. Her chest constricted as if being seized by a strong hand. She forced her hands to keep moving, down Becca's body, to the holster at her side. Her gun was missing, and blood soaked her uniform, Hess's blade was buried in her chest.

Another death on her hands.

She'd lied to Hess. While divers had searched the lake, they hadn't recovered the baby's body, hadn't found a blanket or pacifier, no sign of the child at all. And yet in telling that tale, she'd set Hess against Becca.

She forced herself to take a breath, then another, trails of smoke lodging in her chest and making her cough. Becca was a murderer. Not only had she taken Kelly's life, she'd helped Hess carry out his revenge. But that didn't excuse what Val had done. She couldn't help being sorry a young woman with so much potential was now gone.

Val shook her head, trying to clear her thoughts. She couldn't think of Becca now. Not her betrayal. Not the way Val had sold her out in return. Right now all she could do was lock Becca in a room with Monica and Tamara and pray that when the time came to pull them out again, to examine what had happened, the actions she'd taken, that she'd be able to still look at herself in a mirror.

Grabbing the knife's handle, she worked it free of Becca's corpse. Precious seconds ticked by, her hand slipping on blood, but finally she had a weapon, the means to protect Lund, a way to stop Hess.

The knife in her left hand, she continued her slow, groping crawl. She could sense him near even before her hand touched him.

The thick texture of canvas. A sodden sweatshirt. A thrumming pulse. A moving body. She skimmed her fingers to his face and into his hair. She'd found him, and he was alive, conscious.

Now she had to get him out of here.

She laid her fingers against his cheek, willing him to stay put, to hold on a little longer. Then she crawled back to Becca. Locating her handcuff keys, she unlocked the bracelet on her own arm and returned to Lund.

She freed his hands, then skimmed her fingers down his torso to the shackles binding his legs. One leg of his turnout pants oozed blood.

Her hands shook so badly, she couldn't unlock the shackle chain. Lund levered himself into a sitting position, joining his hands with hers, between the two of them, they wrestled his legs free.

She wasn't sure how damaged his leg was or how well he could move. Unable to ask, she moved back to hands and knees and started inching her way back to the main entrance.

Lund fell in behind her, one hand clamped to her ankle as if performing a search and rescue drill, dragging the injured limb behind.

Almost there.

They reached the door, and Val struggled to her feet to release the lock. She pulled the first door, pushed the second, and helped Lund out into the night.

The air was quiet outside and shockingly cold. She scooped in breath after breath, each exhalation fogging in front of her.

Lund rested on one hip, his hair drenched. Dark circles cupped his eyes. Soot smudged his face. From the look of his turnout pants, he'd lost a significant amount of blood. "We made it," he said, his voice barely a hoarse whisper.

"We made it," echoed Val.

The town was still, as if deserted. No movement. No lights. Low creaks and pops sounded around them, branches swaying and breaking under the weight of ice, trees not able to bear the pressure any longer.

She shivered, her muscles jerking uncontrolled. She was soaked to the skin, like her night in the river, only this time Lund couldn't pull her from the chill. He was submerged right with her. She prayed Grace had been able to reach help.

"Why did you come back?"

She looked into Lund's brown eyes, wondering how he, of all people, could ask that question. "Why did you set fire to the cubicle right behind you?"

He gave her an attempt at a smile. "Blue canary."

"At least I didn't get myself shot."

"Go. Bring back help."

"Grace already did. Someone should be here soon."

But they didn't hear the wail of a siren. They didn't hear voices drifting from houses nearby. They only heard the otherworldly snap of falling trees and limbs groaning in the wind.

Something crunched behind them, a footfall breaking through ice-crusted snow.

"I was wondering what took you so long."

Val tightened her grip on the knife, then turned to look into those cold eyes. "You killed your own daughter."

"Justice." He glared down at her. In his hand, he held Becca's gun.

"That's where you're wrong," she said.

She wanted to hurt him, wound him. Before she died, she wanted to strike back and make him bleed. "We dragged the lake where Kelly was found, but we never recovered a body. Your baby might still be alive. He probably is. But you just killed the only person who knew where he was."

Hess didn't move. His expression never changed. He simply stared at her, at Lund, then he raised the gun.

"Aunt Val!"

Grace raced down the street toward them, a blanket clutched around her shoulders. The silhouettes of others followed her, but Val couldn't focus on them. All she could see was her precious niece.

Melissa's daughter. Her most important thing.

Dixon Hess's lips crooked into a smile, those teeth, those eyes. He turned his head toward Grace, then swung his body, leading with the gun.

Val didn't realize she'd scrambled to her feet until she was running, launching herself. A scream shattered in her ears as she plunged the knife into Hess's back. She pummeled him, slamming her fists against head and shoulders until his knees folded and both of them crumpled to the ice.

Chapter
Thirty

Val found Lund at Rossum Park. He was standing on the pea gravel trail that snaked around the water, crutches canted under his arms, leg encased in an immobilizer. Out on the lake, a boat bobbed at the point where ice met open water, the bright flags of divers dancing on gentle waves.

She glanced at the only other car in the lot, one of Lund's fellow firefighters leaning on the hood, cradling a cup in his hands. The scent of coffee drifted on the cold air. He nodded to her, and she nodded back. Obviously he was giving Lund some time alone.

Maybe she should, too.

She put her hands on the wheel, neither restarting the car and heading back to the temporary police station set up in the public library's meeting room nor pulling the key from the ignition. She had a lot to tell Lund. They'd discovered blood in the basement of his in-laws' old dairy farm. Techs from the state crime lab had been there all morning, but Val already knew the blood belonged to Tamera Wade. They'd even found a needle and thread.

There were other things, too, even more pressing.

And at least one couldn't wait.

Pushing past nerves, she got out of the car. She closed the door, and he turned around.

He didn't smile, didn't give her any sign of welcome at all. Instead they just looked at one another, communicating without her really understanding how.

Maybe that's how it worked when you've gone through hell together and come out on the other side.

She walked up the trail, meeting him by the lake. She didn't say hello or ask how he was. Instead, she simply said. "He's going to live."

"I'm sorry to hear that."

"At least it will be in prison."

He looked as beat up as she did and only half as beat up as she felt. But he was standing. Walking. Alive.

And for that, she was profoundly grateful.

He'd been in the hospital for only a day. The gunshot, while painful, hadn't caused permanent damage. While she'd visited his room, they hadn't talked. It had seemed too soon, everything too raw. She'd just sat in a chair by his bed, and they'd listened to one another breathe.

He and Grace had been different. They'd made plans to hang out, Grace promising to teach him to ride once his leg healed. Lund swearing to take her fishing once the lake thawed in the spring.

But although Val's head was bursting with things she wanted to tell him, explanations she hoped he'd understand, she'd felt they both needed time to be alive. To settle.

Or maybe she was just afraid all the explanations in the world couldn't set things right. "I have better news. Oneida is going to make it, too."

"I'm glad."

"She says she might only have one kidney, but it works, so what the hell. And then she told me I looked tired and wanted me to take her hospital bed."

He gave her a smile.

"Oh, and I talked to Kasdorf."

"He's awake?"

"This morning. It took a lot of convincing, but he gave me a statement. And I have it on video."

He shot her a questioning glance, brows hunkered low over brown eyes.

"He told me how soldiers came into his home. Foreign soldiers dressed to look like firefighters."

"That's a new one."

She pointed across the lake at the forest preserve. "He also told me he was up on that ridge when Becca forced Kelly onto the ice. You're officially cleared, no matter what that planted tissue suggests."

He frowned out at the woods, as if he no longer cared, as if his mind was far away.

She knew what he needed to hear, and she was more than relieved she could provide it. "He also swears Becca took the baby with her when she left."

A muscle twitched along his jaw. "You should have told me. About the baby."

"I couldn't …" She shook her head. She couldn't make excuses. There were none. "I'm sorry."

"I don't believe him."

"Hess?"

"I don't believe the baby is his. I think Kelly knew it, too. I think that's why she left, to protect him from Hess."

Val didn't know what to say. At best, Kelly willingly went along with framing Hess for murder. At worst, she helped Schneider dispose of her aunt's corpse. Lund had been married to her. He loved her. Maybe he still did. She could understand him wanting to think the best of his wife. But Val wasn't willing to go along with his tender portrait, at least not without evidence to back it up. "You think the baby could be yours?"

He turned away from the divers who were searching for something that wasn't there. "Yes."

"You're going to look for him."

"I'm going to find him."

"Lund …"

"I would appreciate any help you could give me."

She nodded. "Of course. I'll do everything I can."

She peered out over the ice. Broken trees rimmed the lake, their shattered frames like something out of a disaster film. And yet the ice still clung to them, sparkling in the sun.

She'd thought she'd found something with Lund for a brief moment, but now the spark between them had changed. She supposed she was okay with that, maybe even a little relieved. She had Grace in her life, and that was hard enough.

Tomorrow she might not be able to lift her foot. The next day, tremors could steal the ability to write or raise a cup of coffee to her lips. No one could say how fast the disease would progress or the severity or the life altering effects. Next month she could be in a wheelchair or she could feel up to going for a horseback ride.

But eventually her symptoms would grow worse. Eventually her body would cease to work.

Lund was a lot like Grace. He liked to help, to rescue others. Even now he couldn't let go of his wife, as if he could rescue her from beyond the grave. Or maybe just have a piece of her in the form of a child who might be his or could just as easily be the son of a killer.

Whatever happened with Lund and Grace, Val knew one thing for certain. While the disease would eventually steal her life, she wasn't willing to steal the lives of those she loved.

Or even those with whom love had been a fleeting hope.

"You back at work?" he asked.

"Not officially, though I'm not suspended, just on leave."

"That's never stopped you before."

"No." As Irony would have it, Pete Olson was acting chief. As irony would also have it, in the past two days, he'd hardly made a move without consulting her. "I'd better get back. You can manage?"

"Dempsey will see I get home. The man's like a mother hen." He reached out his hand as if to touch hers, then let it drop to his side. "Going home to Grace?"

"Speaking of mother hens?" She wanted to touch him. She wanted to stay. Instead she took a step toward the car. Then another. "We're driving the Nova to Chicago."

"Whether your friend wants it back or not?"

"Oh, she loves this car. She just doesn't want to admit it." She forced a smile to her lips. "Take care of yourself, Lund."

"You too, Chief. You too."

She walked back to the car, pushing her thoughts and feelings about Lund behind the closed door with all her other phantoms. Someday she'd have to pull them out, one by one, and examine them. Someday she'd have to come to terms with what she'd done and who she'd loved and how she'd let them down.

Someday.

Today she would focus on Grace.

Epilogue

Lund had to tell her. No matter the outcome, she deserved his thanks.

He'd already tried the refurbished police station, and then he'd checked her house. That left only one place she and Grace could be on this warm spring day, and he already knew the way.

Wind rustled in trees just getting their buds. The air smelled of mud, horse manure and green sprouts of April grass.

He found her in the barn, running a brush over a horse's back. Clumps of shed hair scattered the concrete driveway.

She stopped brushing and turned to face him. "Hi."

"Hi. You look good." He wasn't fibbing. Her hair was pulled back in that business way she seemed to prefer, but dark circles no longer cupped her eyes, instead energy sparkled in them like the sun off Lake Loyal.

"You look good, too. Come to see Grace?"

Her lips pinched a little, and he regretted the awkwardness between them. Unfortunately, a lot had happened in the years they'd known one another, and sometimes you couldn't go back. "I want to thank you."

Val had discovered the baby with Becca's college roommate. The woman had believed she was babysitting while Becca was on vacation.

"You got the tests back?" Val asked.

He nodded.

She watched him, not speaking, as if wanting to read the outcome in his eyes before she dared ask.

"He's not mine."

For a second, he thought he saw tears glossing her eyes. "I'm so sorry."

"Don't be. I had to know. Now I do."

She nodded.

"He's being adopted by a good family. Hess won't be able to reach him. He should have a good life."

"I hope so. I'm just … I regret not telling you right away."

"I know." He should follow with assurances that it was all okay, but he couldn't manage. Not yet. Maybe not for a while. "I appreciate you finding him. That meant a lot to me."

She nodded. "I know things aren't going to be the same between us, and I want you to know I understand. I agree it's for the best. I'm just glad to see you."

"I'm glad to see you, too."

A swallow darted through the barn, wings fluttering. The horse pawed the concrete with a steel-shod hoof.

"Grace is out riding. She'd love to say hi."

He let out a breath. It was good to get their regrets out in the open, but he was relieved to turn to an easier topic. "I didn't see her out there."

"She's on the trails in the woods. You'll have to ride out to find her. Think the leg's up to it?"

"Riding a horse, huh?"

"What do you think?"

It carried a risk, a challenge. And God knew he was a sucker for that particular adrenaline rush. "Only if you go with me."

She gave him a smile, a wonderful sight to see. "Only if you help saddle them up."

"Bring 'em on."

Saddling two horses was more challenging than he'd imagined, but Val was an expert. Her fingers flew, adjusting and buckling, one hand as adept as the other. Soon he was standing out in the warm sun with a fully saddled horse. "Now what do I do?"

"Stand at the horse's shoulder and put your left foot in the stirrup."

He did as she said. "Check."

"Now grab the horn with your left hand and the cantle with your right, and swing your leg over." To demonstrate, she mounted her horse.

Getting on his was a little tougher than she made it look, but finally he was sitting on the horse's back. "The view up here is nice. Maybe I'll quit the fire department and become a cowboy."

She went over how to tell the horse to start and stop and turn. And they started walking away from the barn, the saddle creaking under him, the smell of horse and fresh air teasing his senses.

"You're doing great," Val said. "Any questions?"

"What do I do if I fall off?"

"Get right back on again."

He wasn't sure if she was talking about horses or the rest of life, but maybe it was all part of the same thing. "I guess that's all any of us can do," he said, and they set off down the trail.

Acknowledgments

Much research went into imagining the world of Val Ryker, and I received a lot of help on the way.

Thank you to the Middleton Police Department, led by Chief Brad Keil, and all the officers who taught the citizens' police academy. Special thanks to Officer Greg Dixon, Officer Dave Kasdorf, and Detective Dave Haselow, who have answered my questions over many years and many books. Long ago I promised to name characters after them, although I'm sure they didn't have these particular characters in mind. Luckily their namesakes in the book are nothing like them.

Thank you to the Middleton Fire Department, led by Chief Aaron Harris, and all the firefighters who taught the citizens' firefighter academy. Special thanks to Battalion Chief / Community Education Specialist Brad Subera, without whom David Lund wouldn't have had a clue how to perform his job.

Thank you to the Dane County Sheriff's Department, led by Sheriff Dave Mahoney, and all the deputies and other professionals who taught the citizens' academy.

Special thanks to Public Information Officer Elise Schaffer.

Research is always the first step, and I had lots of help bringing the book to fruition. Special thanks to J.A. Konrath, Maria Konrath, Blake Crouch, and my mom Carol Voss, who has been my sounding board from the beginning … literally.

Of course, acknowledgments aren't complete without thanking my husband John Lund Peterson and our two sons for not minding that I live in imaginary worlds.

And I have to throw in an extra dose of thanks to Wisconsin's terrific public employees. Police, firefighters, teachers, snow plow drivers, correctional officers, and the list goes on. Without you not only would this book not work, but the state of Wisconsin wouldn't either. I'll march with you anytime.

About the Author

A Rita Award nominee and Daphne du Maurier Award winner, Ann Voss Peterson has written 25 romantic suspense novels for Harlequin Intrigue, and now writes thrillers on her own and Codename: Chandler spy thrillers with J.A. Konrath for Thomas & Mercer. This English-creative writing major worked as a bartender, a horse show groom and a professional window washer before publishing her first novel. She has over three million books in print all over the world. Ann lives in Wisconsin with her family.

Made in the USA
Charleston, SC
23 April 2013